Fortuna

a

Family

By Katy Sloop Roberts

Luna and Fortuna Series:

Mario and The Stones

Luna and Fortuna

Fortuna Finds
a
Family

Happy Reading Team Hernandez!

Katy Roberts

Katy Sloop Roberts

Illustrated by Dan Dye

Dan Dye ♡

Dedicated to my mom,

Anne Dye Sloop

*I lack adequate words
to express how much I love you,
how much I admire you,
and how grateful I am
to be your daughter and your friend.*

"For I know the plans I have for you," declares the Lord, "plans to prosper you and not harm you, plans to give you hope and a future."

Jeremiah 29:11

Luna's Italia

Table of Contents

Chapter 1
Happy Birthday

"You are as black as a moonless night sky *la mia bella ragazza*, my beautiful girl," Mother Cat meowed to me, the first of her three kittens born that September morning under the city butcher shop. "You are a very special cat with all black fur!" Mother Cat touched her nose to mine and paused. "*Ti amo*, I love you," she meowed softly.

Within minutes my two brothers were born. Mother Cat purred loudly again.

"*Tre gattini!* Three kittens! *Buon compleanno carissimi*, happy birthday, dear ones. I am very happy to meet you," she meowed while she bathed us.

"*Allora, gattini*, you two are very handsome," she proudly complimented my brothers. "You are striped like a strong tiger," she purred to the kitten on my right. "And you look like a sleek leopard with all of those spots," she admired the kitten on my left.

I could not see Mother Cat because like all kittens, I was born with my eyes closed, but I listened intently and curiously to every word. *"What are tigers and leopards?"* I wondered.

"Benvenuti gattini, welcome kittens, to the most wonderful land in the world, *Italia,* Italy! In *Italia,* you will smell and taste *fantastico* food, hear beautiful music, see high rocky mountains and clear blue seas. You will meet many friendly, energetic people. But for now, we need to sleep. I am exhausted."

Mother Cat kissed each of our foreheads with a lick of her bristly, pink tongue. My brothers and I snuggled tightly together in our basket home. Mother Cat curled around us like a crescent moon. Several hours later I woke to the sound of human voices above us.

"Who is that talking Mother Cat?" I purred inquisitively. I had so many questions. "Are they some of the friendly people we will meet?" I asked between swallows of warm milk.

Mother Cat did not answer me, she just continued to softly purr as she nursed us. When I finished, she washed my face before carefully stepping out of the basket, "I will return shortly. Do not worry," she whispered.

My brothers fell back to sleep almost immediately. I felt the steady rise and fall of their tiny ribs next to me as they dreamed, but my mind was too active to sleep.

"Where is Mother Cat going? When is she coming

back?" I wondered. Finally, I heard a soft thump noise and after a minute, I smelled her.

"I'm glad you are back, Mother Cat. Where did you go? Who did you see? What did you eat? Your breath smells *fantastico!*" I purred in rapid succession.

"Shhh, *mia gattina nera*, my black kitten, not so fast," Mother Cat laughingly purred. She licked the top of my head three times before continuing.

"I went to the back door of the butcher shop. The butcher is a kind man. He gives me meat every day; we have been friends for a long time. I will take you to meet him when you and your brothers are older."

"Can we go *domani*, tomorrow?" I asked full of excitement to make friends.

"Patience little cat, you are not even one day old! You cannot stand up yet. Trust me, you are exactly where you are supposed to be. You are right here with me," she meowed as she licked my forehead again.

"Mother Cat, I want to meet the kind butcher soon. When I am grown up, I am going to have human friends, just like you," I purred confidently.

"I'm sure you will, *ragazza mia*, my girl."

Swish, swish, swish.

Repeated a soothing sound above us. I was tired, but my curiosity was stronger.

"Mother Cat? What is that swish, swish, swishing sound?" I meowed with a yawn.

"It is a broom, my curious *gattina*."

"I like that sound. It is relaxing," I replied. I yawned and kneaded my tiny black paws against Mother Cat's stomach before nestling close to her.

"*Sì, sì, sì*, yes, right now it is," she agreed.

"What is a broom?" I meowed sleepily. But Mother Cat was already asleep.

Chapter 2
Breakfast with the Butcher

"*Buongiorno gattini*, good morning, kittens. Today you are nine days old. *Allora*, you are growing so quickly," Mother Cat meowed as she gently nudged us. "*Perfetto*, perfect! You can open your eyes now! Soon, when you are a little steadier on your feet, I will lift you out of the basket, and you can explore the space under this building."

"I want to explore now, Mother Cat!" I responded eagerly. I sat up straight to show her how big I was. "I also want to meet the kind butcher, see the mountains and the sea, taste delicious food, but most of all, I want to play with children like the ones in your stories!" I meowed in one breath.

"*Ragazza mia*, my girl," Mother Cat purred.

"Try to be patient. You have much to learn."

A week later my brothers and I mastered walking in a line behind Mother Cat, but she still said we were not ready to venture from the space below the butcher shop. We played hide and seek with each other and chased unsuspecting lizards that crawled under the building, but I was ready to have adventures.

Three long weeks later, Mother Cat finally said we were ready to see a little of the city, Pudoia.

"*Andiamo, gattini*, let's go, kittens. The butcher's wife just left for her daily trip to the bakery. Now is our best chance to visit the kind butcher. Line up, *per favore*, please," she instructed, looking both excited and nervous.

I did not wait for her to repeat herself. At last, we were going out! I briskly ran and stood behind Mother Cat. "Hurry up," I meowed impatiently to my brothers, who always walked leisurely.

"This part is loose," Mother Cat explained as she touched a particular board with her paw. "Push it firmly with your head and walk forward. I will wait for you on the street." Mother Cat disappeared behind the flimsy board.

The board moved easily, and I entered the world beyond our home for the first time. As my eyes adjusted to the morning sunlight, I stretched my back into a high arch.

"*Stai attenta, cara,* be careful, dear! You will frighten people arching your back like that," Mother Cat warned me as she looked up and down the street.

"*Perché, why?*" I questioned, wanting to know how a simple stretch of my small body could frighten a big human, but she walked ahead without answering me.

"Come along, *gattini.* I want us to enjoy a nice breakfast with the butcher before his wife returns."

As I hurried to catch up, my little black nose breathed in wonderful aromas.

"*È carne*, it is meat," Mother Cat meowed. She licked her lips.

My stomach growled for the fresh meat. When we reached the back steps, my brothers and I climbed over one another to reach the glorious smells first. Mother Cat, however, swiftly grabbed us one at a time by the backs of our necks. She sat us down in a row on the dusty street.

"We must be nice guests. Sit politely while I let the butcher know we are here." In one swift leap, she jumped up the steps.

"Meow, meow," she sweetly cried.

"*Buongiorno!* Good morning!" the butcher called to us in a deep, jolly voice. He wiped his hands on his long apron. "Who have you brought with you today? Why you are a mother! *Molto bene*, well done, Mother Cat! *I tuoi gattini sono bellissimi*, your kittens are beautiful," he said with a broad smile. "Now I understand why you have been extra hungry," the butcher said, still smiling.

He stepped back inside and returned a few moments later carrying a plate. Mother Cat approached him confidently. He scratched behind her ear before giving her some meat. Next, he put a stack of pink sliced meat on the bottom step for me and my brothers to share.

"*Mortadella per te e la tua famiglia*, bologna for you and your family," he said with a wink. "It is my favorite. I hope you like it too."

9

My brothers and I instantly surrounded the meat. Immediately, we began to eat, but they pushed me back.

Seeing my predicament as the smallest kitten, the kind butcher chuckled. He knelt on the top step with the plate of *mortadella*. I quickly hopped up the stairs.

The *mortadella* was pink like my brothers' noses. It was soft and rich with fatty flavor. I loved

it. *"I hope we come every day for colazione con il macellaio, breakfast with the butcher,"* I thought with delight.

"Run along," the kind butcher said to Mother Cat. I was still enjoying the tasty meat. My brothers were licking the steps for remaining meaty juices. "My wife will be back soon. As you know, you should not be here when she returns."

With a loud purr, Mother Cat instructed us to follow her. For once, I was the last to line up. I sat daintily on the top step with my tail wrapped around my front paws hoping the butcher would scratch behind my ear.

"You especially better keep this little one out of her sight," he cautioned as he pointed to me.

"Perché, why," I meowed. "I am just a tiny kitten, even smaller than my brothers, how could I ever bother a human?"

"Sì, sì, sì, yes," Mother Cat meowed. *"Andiamo a casa,* let's go home."

"But I don't want to go home," I purred in disagreement. "I want to stay and play with the kind butcher. I also want more of his delicious meat!"

"Anch'io, me too!" meowed both of my

orange brothers at almost the same time.

"*Domani*, tomorrow we will come again," replied Mother Cat. "I am proud of you, *gattini*. You behaved nicely on your first outing. Meat for breakfast will help you grow into strong cats who can run and jump quick as a flash of lightning and climb as high as the tallest bell towers, but we must not be greedy or overstay our welcome."

Mother Cat sauntered toward the entrance to our home. My brothers followed, but I remained. I was still hoping the kind butcher would scratch behind my ear like he greeted Mother Cat earlier. I sat with my head stretched up looking directly at him. Finally, he seemed to understand. He knelt placing his knees next to my front paws and scratched behind my left ear.

His touch was different from Mother Cat's licks, but also very satisfying. I leaned into his hand and almost lost my balance when he stopped scratching my neck. He towered over me like a giant as he stood, but I was not afraid. I was happy to have my first human friend.

"*Grazie*, thank you," I purred as I rubbed my

cheek against his brown leather shoe. *"I can hardly wait to come again tomorrow and the next day and every day,"* I thought happily, as he patted my head again.

"Run along now," he said. He nudged me gently in the direction of my family. I jumped down the steps one at a time. My little feet made only the slightest pitter-pat sounds on the wooden stairs.

Chapter 3
The Butcher's Wife

"Mother Cat, is it time for breakfast with the butcher?" we pleaded again.

We were busy, playful eight-week-old kittens. My favorite game was hide and seek. The many discarded boxes and baskets under the shop were perfect hiding places for a black kitten to win hide and seek. I outwitted my brothers almost daily.

We played together for hours each day, and we were also growing rapidly which meant we were always hungry. We craved the butcher's delicious meat. Yesterday, he gave us a new treat called *prosciutto crudo*, salted ham. I liked it even more than *mortadella*. It smelled so good!

Mother Cat, however, said, "No. Please stop asking. Be patient! You can hear the butcher's wife above us as well as I can. We must wait." Mother Cat sighed and yawned before lying down in our basket.

I knew she was right. I had never seen the butcher's wife, and I did not want to see her. She yelled at the children who came into the shop with their parents. Sometimes she even yelled at the kind butcher. She was not nice like her husband. When I was a newborn kitten I thought the sound of her broom was soothing. Now I knew the swish, swish, swish meant I would hear her yelling too. I do not like loud noises. *"Perché, why are some humans so noisy?"* I wondered.

Cats are quiet. We only make soft gentle noises. We move quietly too. I am especially good at walking without making any noise. Mother Cat says I move like the night air as black cats do best.

I am ready to meet more people, but not loud mean ones like the butcher's wife. Mother Cat tells us stories at night about her many human friends. My favorite stories are about children. I have not met any children yet, but I hope to soon. I want to play with them. I hear them in the store above and on the street too. They make smaller noises with their feet than bigger humans, and they are playful just like me.

I have decided I am going to have a human family. They will have lots of children. They will feed me good meats and scratch behind my ears just like the kind butcher does. I feel warm inside and out when the butcher pets me.

As I was imagining my future family, Mother Cat called us to line up. We scampered behind her and pushed our way through the loose board one at a time. I was first, of course. I am always first. I waited in the street with Mother Cat for my brothers to appear. Just as the orange tip of my striped brother's tail cleared the board, I heard a mean voice. It was the butcher's wife! She was on the back steps of the shop.

"*Gatti? Gatti?* Cats living under my shop?" she yelled angrily.

"What should we do?" we meowed in alarm.

"*Presto*, quick! Go back behind the board!

Presto, presto, gattini! Via adesso, go now!" Mother Cat urgently commanded.

The butcher's wife approached us holding her broom like a knight ready to swing his sword.

"*Via subito*, away immediately!" she yelled. She swung the broom in our direction. "*No non sotto!* No, not under there! Customers will think the shop is infested with rodents if they see cats living under the building. *Andate via*! Go now!" She yelled as my brothers and I scrambled to escape behind the loose board.

Mother Cat hissed at the butcher's wife until we were safely under the shop. The fur on her back stood straight up, and the fur on her tail stuck out in every direction. It was as fat as a big sausage.

The butcher's wife swung her broom again, but Mother Cat was too quick. She jumped forward, straight through the mean woman's legs, darted under her skirt, and ran quickly around the far corner of the building.

Under the shop we were scared. I knew the butcher's wife was not a nice woman, but I never thought she might try to hurt us.

"Where is Mother Cat? Why didn't she come with us? What do we do now? I'm hungry!" my brothers whimpered.

WHAP! WHAP! WHAP!

A sharp, loud noise echoed through our home. The butcher's wife hammered the loose board in place, trapping us. My brothers cried harder.

"Shhhhhhhh," I meowed. "*Silenziate!* Be quiet! *Ascoltate*, listen. I think I hear something."

When they finally quieted, and the ringing in my ears stopped, I heard Mother Cat calling us.

"*Gattini, gattini,*" she meowed to us from the other side of the shop. We sprinted across the dirt floor, jumping over our hide-and-seek boxes. We found Mother Cat, but she was in the busy street.

"*Presto gattini,* quickly kittens! Squeeze through right here," she urged as she reached her grey paw under a broken board. "I know you will fit. I cannot come to you, I am too big."

"*Molto bene, ragazza mia,* well done, my girl," she said as I crawled under first. I was covered in dirt, but I did not care.

"*Presto,* hurry," she urged my brothers. "You

18

must come to me — *presto* before the butcher's wife sees us," she panted nervously.

They obeyed. Mother Cat did not hesitate. She ran across the street toward the bakery, skillfully darting between and around the people who were out shopping. We followed her the best we could, but we had only been in the street at night when it was quiet. It was hard to know exactly where to run so no one stepped on us. I led. My brothers followed.

Once we all crossed the street safely, Mother Cat slowed to a trot, but she did not stop until we reached a curved alley with arches overhead.

"*Venite qui, gattini*, come here, kittens," she purred. "I am grateful you are not hurt."

"What do we do now?" my brothers cried.

"We will rest today while the streets are busy. Tonight I will teach you to hunt. There are always mice in these alleys." That night with Mother Cat's help, we each caught a mouse for dinner.

"*Bene, gattini*. I am proud of you. You were brave today, and now you are mighty hunters too." Mother Cat laid down and purred for us to come close. Exhausted from a dangerous day, we snuggled together, I under Mother Cat's chin and my brothers next to me along her ribs.

Early the next morning after we hunted, caught, and ate mice, Mother Cat gathered us together. She took a deep breath.

"*Miei dolci gattini,* my sweet kittens, you are big enough now to go off on your own," she explained.

"I will miss you, Mother Cat," I meowed, "but I am very excited to see what is beyond *questa città,*

this city. I want to see Italy's blue seas and high mountains. Most of all, I want to find a family with lots of children who will play with me every day."

"*Bene, ragazza mia.* I am glad you know what you want, but be careful, my eager *gattina.* You must try to be patient. You will find the right family, though it may take you time to find them." Mother Cat kissed my forehead with her bristly pink tongue.

"*Sì*, yes, Mother Cat. *Ci proverò,* I will try," I promised as I stood up and nuzzled her.

My brothers sat next to each other, very close together. I could tell they were nervous about leaving Mother Cat. The black circles in their green eyes were huge.

"*Addio*, good-bye," I meowed to them.

"Off you go now, *la mia bellissima gattina nera*, my beautiful black kitten. I know *la famiglia perfetta*, the perfect family is waiting for you."

"*Grazie*, thank you, Mother Cat," I purred. Mother Cat and I exchanged slow blinks, which means 'I love you,' in cat language. I walked out of the alley with my head and tail held high.

Chapter 4
On My Way

I was more excited than nervous walking by myself on the street. I was on my way to find a human family of my very own. A family who would scratch behind my ears, feed me meat, and play with me. Happy thoughts of my future family floated through my head like butterflies as I walked the cobbled streets of Pudoia.

I paused in front of the blacksmith shop. Warm air flowed from the open front door. The blacksmith stood inside near a fire. He did not look like the family I imagined.

He had a scruffy white beard and white hair on his head too. I had never seen someone so old.

"Could old people be as playful and fun as the children in Mother Cat's stories?" I wondered as I watched him. He stooped over a table next to a roaring fire. He held a long black rod into the flames. When he pulled the rod from the fire, it glowed bright red!

BANG, bang, bang, bang!

He hammered the rod until it turned black again. Wiping sweat from his forehead, he raised his eyes. We looked at each other for a few seconds, I with my little head cocked to one side curious about his work, and he with a sweaty grin. He looked friendly, but I did not like the loud noises he made with his tools. When he put the rod into the fire again, I continued on my way.

I walked into Pudoia's *piazza*, town square, just as the bells rang seven times. I like the bells. They are noisy if you are too close to the tower, but they play beautiful tones in melodic rhythms. Mother Cat said the bells help the humans stay on schedule. I do not know what a schedule is, but I don't think cats have them.

I did know the bells meant the *piazza* would soon be filled with people. Even though I wanted to meet new friends, being on my own for the very first time, I did not want to navigate the busy *piazza* without Mother Cat.

"*I will walk to the far side of the city where it is not as crowded,*" I concluded, "*but which way should I go?*"

I trotted toward the fountain in the center of the square to get a drink of water and think. My little black padded paws made soft thumping noises on the cobbles as I ran. A flock of speckled brown birds scattered, taking flight as I crossed the *piazza*.

I liked this fountain because at its center was a statue of a friendly-looking man holding a bird in his cupped hands. He wore a long robe and sandals. The water flowed over his feet. Bird sculptures adorned the round rim of the fountain which was easily ten times my height.

"Nrrr-uuu-mm-p," I sang in my throat with ascending notes before I jumped. My song gives me confidence when I have to make a big leap. I landed perfectly on the fountain's edge.

The white marble was cool and slick because it was wet, but I did not fall. I am good at balancing. I walked on the curved fountain rim, stepping over the marble birds until I reached the place where the water flowed into the fountain. Last week when we visited the *piazza* at night with Mother Cat, I discovered the water tasted best from this spot.

As I enjoyed a long drink, I watched a man. "Meow," I greeted him.

"*Buongiorno*," he said, reaching his hand into a cloth bag. He tossed a handful of seeds on the ground for the birds. "You have picked the best fountain in Pudoia. He pointed to the statue in the center of the fountain. "Saint Francis of Assisi is a protector of animals," he said as he smiled at me.

I walked toward the man, but he held up his palm. "No, stop. Cats make my eyes itch. If I touch you I will be miserable for hours."

"*That's odd*," I thought. "*Touching people does not make me itchy.*"

I drank more of the refreshing water while I watched the man and the birds. When the birds finished the seeds, they flew away. The man left too. I was alone to think. "*They know where they are going, but I do not.*"

"*This water must come from somewhere far away,*" I

concluded. *"It smells and tastes fresher than this city. I will follow the water out of Pudoia and see where it leads."*

People were beginning to fill the *piazza*. It was time for me to go. First, I followed the long, narrow trough connected to the fountain. As it reached the corner of the *piazza*, it became level with the rise of the street. I walked on the edge of the waterway listening to the rushing water.

"I like the sound of water," I thought. *"Fish live in water. Mother Cat says fresh fish is the best cat food in the whole world. Perhaps I will choose a family who lives at the sea, so I can eat fish every day!"*

I was so focused on my new idea before I knew it, I was high above Pudoia. "I can see the butcher shop from here." I meowed. "I am glad to be far away from the butcher's wife, but I will miss the kind butcher and his delicious meats. I wonder if Mother Cat will still visit him?"

I started to feel sad as I thought about Mother Cat, but I repeated her encouraging words in my head until I felt better. *"You will find the perfect family."*

I looked down at Pudoia once more. "I will search until I find *la famiglia perfetta*, the perfect family," I meowed. With my head and my tail held high, I ran up the road next to the stream.

Later when the sun was high in the blue sky, I stopped for a rest in the shade of a tall tree. The sound of the stream was very soothing. I fell asleep almost immediately, but I soon woke to a frightful growling noise. At first, I thought it was a wild animal. Thankfully, it was only my stomach. *"What a relief,"* I thought. *"I will hunt as Mother Cat taught me."*

I crouched low. I stayed perfectly still, except for my eyes and ears. The birds sang above me. *"I could never eat a bird who sings beautiful songs,"* I thought. *"I will have to wait for a mouse to come along."* I waited a long time. I did not see or hear any mice.

Finally, a big brown grasshopper jumped with one long leap into the road. I responded with one quick leap. I pounced, landing directly on top of the grasshopper. It tasted terrible, but my stomach stopped making noises.

While I finished my crunchy meal, I heard another noise. It sounded far away. I fixed my eyes, concentrating ahead on the road, but I did not see anything. The noise became louder as I continued walking, but I still did not see anything. It reminded me of the bells in Pudoia, but it was not as rhythmic or as pleasant. It was a clanging sound.

"I wish that clanging noise would stop! I can't hear the singing birds very well." There were so many more birds along this road than in the city. *"I wonder what they are all called?"* The birds were many beautiful colors, and they each sang their own song. *"I love bird music,"* I thought. *"Perhaps I will find a family who lives near a forest with lots of songbirds."*

Eventually, as my shadow became long, the clanging noise became less frequent. *"I hope, I will learn what is making that noise tomorrow."*

The dark grey stones paving the road were warm from the sun. They heated the little black pads on my paws, but as the sun sank behind the trees, the air chilled quickly. I walked until the crescent moon rose high in the dark sky.

"I am tired," I meowed.

I chose a bush and crawled under its low branches. The ground was covered with thick green moss. I kneaded the squishy moss with my front paws, turned once in a circle, and curled into a tight ball with my tail tucked under my chin.

Chapter 5
The Noisy Parade

CLANG,…CLANG,……CLANG!

I woke suddenly. The clanging noise sounded as if it was right on top of me. My ears twitched; my eyes widened; shivers ran down my spine to the tip of my tail, which was at least four times its usual size.

CLANG, clang,…clang, CLANG!

The noise erupted from large, shiny brass bells around the necks of enormous brown and white animals! They did not look like cats, even though they had four legs and long tails. Their legs were knobby like old tree trunks. Their tails swished back and forth, very different from the movement of my own tail.

I was nervous because I had never seen an animal this big. I was fascinated. The shiny bells jangled as the animals walked. I watched with wide eyes.

"Mmmooooooo!" A huge animal called in my direction. It looked straight at me with large, brown eyes. It appeared to be curious too.

"*Perhaps it has never seen a kitten,*" I thought.

The animals followed each other down the road toward Pudoia. Their hooves made heavy clomping noises on the stone road. I did not want one of them to step on me, so I remained under the bush. When the last animal in the noisy parade passed, two men followed.

"I am glad we are almost to the city so I can rest my feet. My feet are sore from walking all the way from *i monti*, the mountains," the short man said to the tall man as they passed me.

Once the road was empty and the clanging noise softened, I emerged. I stretched. First, I stretched both of my front legs forward with my back sagging like the backs of the mooing animals, then I stretched into a high arch. It felt good to stretch after being still for a long time.

I sat in the middle of the road taking my bath. The morning dew on the paving stones sparkled in the sunlight causing me to see spots. I blinked my eyes until the spots disappeared; that is when I saw a wooden sign at a fork in the road just ahead.

Curious to see what I could learn from the sign, I ran to it. I could not read the words, but just like the signs in the city, it had both pictures and words.

"*If I go one way, I will go toward il mare, the sea. If I go the other way, I will go to i monti, the mountains,*" I determined. I thought for a minute.

"*Fantastico!* I am going to the sea, the beautiful blue Italian sea, where the fish live!" I meowed with confident excitement.

My stomach was growling again, but the thought of eating fish energized me. I trotted along the road eager to eat fish, and most of all, to make new friends.

I did not walk far before I noticed the air was different. It tasted wet and salty.

"*Perfetto! I must be getting close!*"

Chapter Six
The Fishing Village

The fishing village smelled and looked nothing like Pudoia. Delicious fishy aromas hung in the humid air, and the buildings were vibrant with colors. Orange, yellow, and pink houses adorned with green shutters covered the cliff above the bright blue sea.

"*Fantastico*! I made it!" I purred happily. "Now I am going to find *pesce a colazione*, fish for breakfast. *Ho fame*, I am hungry," I meowed.

Even though the houses blocked my view of the sea as I entered the village, I easily navigated toward the water. I ran down the steep road until I reached flat ground. The sea was just beyond behind a stone wall.

Big, loud, white birds swooped down and called noisily above me. I felt a rush of wind from their long wings as they flew over my head. *"I hope they are hungry for fish, not a kitten,"* I thought. I walked close to the buildings, hoping to be invisible to the squawking sea birds.

I forgot about the birds as soon as I stood on the sea wall and saw the beach. The blue water glistened like millions of sapphires. Long skinny wooden boats lined the sandy beach. Fishermen were hauling baskets of fish out of their boats and onto wooden carts.

"Perfetto!" I meowed hungrily looking at the mounds of fish. I jumped up onto the closest cart and hungrily licked a small silvery fish. Before I could lick the salty little fish a second time, a big hairy arm scooped me up and plopped me down into the sand.

"No, no, no go! *Vai via!* Go away!" A man with leathery tan skin said to me in a stern voice as he clapped his hands loudly.

I backed up, hiding under his cart. I tried to make myself small by crouching low in the sand, but the man leaned down and yelled at me again to leave. "Get out of here! You will bring bad luck to my boat!"

I crawled out from the far side of his cart and walked slowly back to the sea wall. *"Surely, someone here will share fish with a hungry kitten,"* I hoped.

As I sat, looking longingly at the many baskets full of fish, a boy with dark brown hair approached. He smiled. *"Buongiorno, gattina,"* he said cheerfully. He placed a shimmery, skinny fish at my front paws. It was the size of a big caterpillar; a perfect size for a hungry kitten. I smelled the little fish. It smelled scrumptious!

"È una sardina, it is a sardine," the boy said as I licked the fish. *"Mio papà,* my dad and I caught hundreds of them this morning. It was a good morning for fishing. The water is calm today. The fish practically jumped into our nets. Papà is very happy." The boy placed three more fish in front of me. I purred because the fish was delicious and because a boy, a real boy, was talking to me.

"He is going to be my best friend," I thought happily. *"I knew I would make friends quickly."*

"*Mia nonna*, my grandmother cooks sardines better than anyone in Portazzurro," the boy said proudly as he brushed his hair away from his eyes.

"*Portazzurro, the blue port. That's a good name for this village,*" I thought.

The boy smiled at me as he continued talking. "I love Nonna's sardines cooked in lemon juice and olive oil, but I see you like them just fine raw." He laughed cheerfully and patted the top of my head as I swallowed the first fish.

I purred as the second fish slid down my throat. "*Grazie, ragazzo, thank you, boy,*" I longed to tell him. I rubbed my cheek against his hip. The boy scratched behind my ear. "*He likes me,*" I thought with delight. I rapidly ate the other two fish.

"Adriano?...*Dove sei?* Where are you?" A deep voice called from down the beach.

"I have to go back to work with *mio padre*, my father. *Ciao, gattina!* Bye, kitten!" the boy said, as he abruptly stood up and jumped into the sand.

The boy ran down the beach. "Wait for me, *ragazzo*," I meowed. I followed him the best I could. It was hard to run through the sand. My paws slipped backward with every step, but I reached the boy at his father's wooden boat a few minutes later. Immediately, I jumped up to the rim of the boat.

"Meow," I said announcing myself. *"Please pet me again and play with me."*

The boy's father turned around. Without taking his eyes off of me he said, "Adriano, c*hi è questo*, who is this?"

"Just a little kitten I found on the beach this morning. She looked hungry. I gave her four of our sardines. Isn't she nice, Papà?"

"She does look *dolce*, sweet, but with that black fur, many people in this village will disagree. You, my son, have work to do." His rough hands moved quickly tying knots in ropes as he spoke.

I thought the ropes looked like a fun toy, but I politely resisted batting them as they dangled from the man's calloused hands.

"No time to play with a kitten today, Adriano. The cart is full and ready. Take the fish into town then go to school. I do not want you to be late."

"*Sì, Papà*, yes, Papà," he obediently answered. He quickly jumped over the edge of the boat and stepped up to the wooden cart full of sardines. He grabbed the handles in both hands and hoisted the cart at an angle making the front wheel roll forward. It looked like a very heavy load for a boy, but Adriano managed. I jumped down from the rim of the fishing boat and trotted behind my new friend. I kept up with him just fine this time.

We did not walk very far before Adriano stopped and spoke to an old man with a crooked back. The man moved his hand up and down, side to side across his chest as he glared at me. "Do not ever bring that black cat with you again," he said sternly. He paused and scowled at me, "Or else," he looked crossly at Adriano, "your father will have to find another fish merchant."

"*Capisco*, I understand, Signore Marinus," Adriano replied politely.

I understood too. Some people did not like me because of my black fur. *How am I supposed to tell the difference between people who like black cats and people who do not?* " I thought feeling bewildered.

Adriano left the fishing cart with the old man. He skipped up the road, through the *piazza*, and into a narrow alley between brightly painted buildings. I followed him, eager to play and have him scratch behind my ear again.

"Adriano is very fast!" I thought as the gap between us quickly widened.

The alley narrowed more between tall colorful buildings as I ran behind Adriano. Soon it was only a passageway of stairs leading up the hill away from the sea. Adriano ran up the stairs two at a time.

"Meowwww," I cried from exhaustion.

Adriano stopped. He rested his hands on his thighs as he breathed heavily. "*Gattina*, I did not know you were still following me! You can't come to *scuola*, school. Wait out here. I will see you later. *Ciao!*" He shook his hand in a hurried wave and bounded up more stairs before disappearing through a large gate.

No longer needing to run, I hopped up one step at a time, resting when I needed a break. Unfortunately, when I reached the school, I could not open the heavy brass-hinged metal gate. I hopped onto a round stone pedestal. "*I will wait right here for Adriano.*" I sat with my tail wrapped around my paws.

Two other children approached from farther up the stairs. They also ran quickly. They did not stop to talk to me. They opened and closed the gate quickly, disappearing inside.

Throughout the morning I heard the happy voices of children. I longed to join them. A whole group of children was almost more than I could have hoped to find on my first day in Portazzurro. "*I hope they come out soon. I am ready to play.*"

41

Bong,…bong,…bong.…

The bells in the *piazza* below rang twelve times. The sound echoed pleasantly on the bright buildings. Moments later the school gate burst open and a flood of children ran past me. Some children went up the stairs, and other children went down. Adriano led the group racing down.

"Wait for me," I meowed as I hopped down the stairs behind the children, but they were too fast for me. When I reached the bottom step, I did not see Adriano. I looked right and left. The whole street was quiet.

My feelings were hurt. Adriano forgot about me. I did not want to be alone. I was here to make friends and find a family. "*It's ok. I will just introduce myself to the next person who walks down this road,*" I decided with optimistic determination. I sat and waited.

My ears twitched at the sound of approaching voices. The conversation sounded jovial. "*They must be happy about fishing like Adriano and his papà. I bet they will be happy to see me since they are in such good moods,*" I thought. I walked with my tail straight up, eager as always to meet a new friend.

As I rounded a turn in the road I saw two men walking shoulder to shoulder. They reminded me of the sea birds the way they flapped their arms as they talked about fishing.

I trotted up to them. "Meow, meow," I announced politely.

The man closest to me turned his head at my greeting, but when he saw me, his happy expression vanished, his eyes widened, and his fingers curled into a tight fist.

"Get out of here devilish *gatto nero*, black cat!" he roared like a lion. He stomped his boot on the stone road with a loud smack. The noise echoed off the buildings.   Frightened and disappointed, I ran back into the school alley where I hid in the shadows.

"They looked friendly and happy, but they did not like me because of my black fur. Some people are nice to me and some are not. What was I to do?" I could no sooner change my fur color than grow fins and swim in the sea like a fish. I sat in the alley feeling confused and sad.

I liked everyone, no matter their age or what

color hair they had, but not everyone liked me. *"How do I know who will be my friend?"* That night I cried myself to sleep.

The next morning I was *molto affamata,* very hungry, and also very determined to learn clues for understanding people.

"Maybe Adriano will be on the beach again this morning," I thought as I retraced my steps from yesterday through the *piazza* toward the sea.

I sat on the sea wall scanning the beach for Adriano. As the sun rose in a bright orange-pink glowing sphere over the watery horizon, boats began to return to shore. *"All of these boats are alike. I hope I don't have to look very long for Adriano's boat because I am ready to eat his good fish."*

Fortunately, I did not have to find Adriano. He found me. *"Buongiorno gattina,"* he chirped from behind me. I see you are back for *colazione,* breakfast. You are in luck. I already took the fish cart to the grouchy old fish merchant. I saved five sardines for you…I hoped you would come back," he said with a smile as he pulled the fish from his pants pocket.

Chapter 7
The Crab, the Children, and Nonna

Adriano sat on the sea wall next to me, his brown curly hair blowing across his eyes. He patted me briefly with his rough, calloused fisherman hands. I purred, grateful for his attention.

"*Uno, due, tre, quattro, cinque*," he said as he counted five sardines and placed them on the sea wall by my paws.

"*Oggi è sabato*, today is Saturday. I do not have to go to school. Papà said I could stay on the beach and play until lunchtime. Do you want to play with me, *gattina*?"

"*Sì, sì, sì!*" I meowed excitedly.

I ate all five fish without looking up. I liked the way the fish tasted and how they slid down my throat. They did not stick in my throat like hairy caterpillars.

"*Andiamo, gattina*! Let's go, kitten! Catch me if you can!" He called over his shoulder as he jumped down into the sand and ran toward the blue water.

"I'll try, Adriano!" I replied with a meow.

I licked my lips clean and jumped off the wall in pursuit. The sand was cold on my little feet. Remembering how hard it was to run in the sand yesterday, I crouched low and leaped. I landed on all four feet and repeated my mighty jumps across the beach to Adriano.

He cheered and clapped as I approached. "*Molto bene, gattina!* Well done, kitten!"

This was a much better way for me to cross the beach. Adriano patted my head, but before I could rub my cheek on his palm, he took off running again. He ran on the wet sloped part of the beach. His bare feet splashed as the gentle waves swept up and faded back rhythmically. I followed him, but the water did not just splash my feet. It splashed my face.

I do not like to have a wet face. I shook my head, sending a small spray of salty water in all directions.

"Maybe I should stay on the dry sand," I thought, *"and leave the water to Adriano. He seems to think it is fun to get wet, but I do not like it."*

I sat down in the cool, dry sand away from the water to wash my face. I licked my left paw and rubbed it against my cheek just as something darted across the sand and into a small hole.

Even though I only saw it out of the corner of my eye for a split second, and I did not know what it was, I was curious. I crouched down and waited. I crouched lower. I remained perfectly still as a good hunter does.

Soon, an odd little animal with a hard shell and eyes on top of its head came partway out of the hole. It paused before fully exiting. My eyes widened as I watched it. It had many jointed legs, and it walked sideways.

I swished the tip of my black tail and wiggled my hips in anticipation of a successful catch. I pounced, landing right in front of the strange, orange creature.

"*What a good hunter I am…*MEOWWWW!!!"

I jumped backward to escape my prey, but it came with me, attached to my right paw. I shook my paw vigorously. The little monster flew high through the air and landed with a splash in the water.

Adriano stood over me laughing with his hands on his sandy knees. He laughed until tears glistened in his brown eyes.

"*Gattina,*" he gasped between laughs. "Don't

you know not to play with *granchi*, crabs?"

I sat in the sand licking my right paw. It did not hurt nearly as much as my pride hurt. I was embarrassed for not knowing about crabs. I tucked my tail under me and stared at the ground, too ashamed to look at Adriano. "*I do not know about crabs because there are no crabs in the city,*" I thought.

"*Ciao,* Adriano," a boy said as he approached us. He looked at me then at Adriano. "Let's play," he said. "The others will join us soon."

After the crab fiasco, the rest of the morning was *perfetta*. Adriano's friends arrived at the beach in pairs. The boys chased each other and played in the waves up to their knees before starting a game with a ball. They expertly kicked the ball to each other while running the length of the beach many times. The girls giggled and jumped backward as the waves touched their toes.

I leaped behind the boys back and forth across the beach until I was exhausted. Adriano eventually became tired too and joined me on the warm sand for a rest.

"In the summer, we swim," he explained. "I

swim almost as well as a fish, but it is too cold to swim in *Novembre*, so we play ball instead."

The beach felt alive with the happy energy and laughter of the children. I felt happy too. Playing with children was exactly what I imagined when I left the city. I did not want the morning to end…it felt like a dream come true. I sat on a large black rock warmed by the sun and closed my eyes contentedly.

Eventually, the girls tired of playing in the waves. They collected shells and smooth, colorful rocks they called *i vetri di mare*, sea glass. They placed the shells and sea glass on the sand in patterns around my rocky perch.

"It looks like the kitten is sitting on a throne!" a girl with long curls said enthusiastically.

"*Sì, sì, sì,*" her friend agreed. "She is a *principessa*, princess!" The girls giggled happily as they twirled in circles around me.

I looked from one girl to the next. "I knew I would make friends," I purred.

When the sun was high in the sky, the crowd of children started to grow smaller. The girl with the long curls picked me up and carried me across the beach. She patted my head as she put me on the sea wall. "*Arrivederci*, goodbye," she said as she skipped toward the *piazza*.

"*Wait for me!*" I wanted to say to her, but I also wanted to wait for Adriano, who was still playing ball. "*Who should I follow home? I like them all! Which child is the best choice to be my family?*" I wondered.

One by one the children ran up the beach into town. Some of them greeted me, but the others ran by without stopping.

Adriano was the last to leave the beach. He carried the ball under one arm. He sat next to me on the sea wall while he brushed sand from his feet. "I don't know if I can keep you, *gattina*, but I will try. Let's go home."

"Home!" I purred as I followed my boy.

I followed Adriano into the *piazza*, past the bell tower, past a church with two enormous lion statues at the entrance, and into a narrow alley that led to a flight of stone stairs. By the time we reached the stairs, I was exhausted.

"Meeooowwww!" I cried to Adriano who was

far ahead of me.

He turned around and jogged back. He picked me up, holding me snuggly against his chest. I felt his heart beating rapidly as he resumed running. "We are almost home for *pranzo*, lunch. *Ho fame*! I'm starving!" he said.

"*Bene, good*," I thought. "*I am hungry too*."

"Here we are," Adriano announced as he kicked open a squeaky wooden gate with one foot.

We entered a small stone courtyard that overlooked the beautiful sea on one side and led to a yellow house with green shutters on the other side. Laundry hung on a line above the courtyard. It cast dancing shadows of pants and shirts on the ground. Adriano dropped the ball, but he kept hold of me as he skipped across the yard, ducked under the billowing laundry, and entered the house.

The kitchen was quiet except for the soft bubbling of simmering pots in the hearth. My stomach growled as I smelled fish. I wiggled to break free from Adriano's grasp, but he held me tightly.

"*Shh, gattina!*" he whispered.

He carried me upstairs and placed me in a

small bedroom.   Then he left, closing the door behind him, trapping me inside.

"Come back," I meowed. "I'm hungry and I want to stay with you." But there was no response.

The one window in the room was cracked open. "Nrrr-uuu-mm-p," I sang as I jumped to the window sill and squeezed into the opening.

I saw colored houses to the right and the left with the blue sea beyond, but even for an agile kitten, it was much too high to jump. Adriano's house was high up on the cliff, and this window was easily twenty meters above the ground. Taking a closer look, I saw a thick vine growing along the wall under the window.   "*I will climb out along the vine and go back to the front door so I can be with Adriano,*" I planned.

Just then I heard Adriano bounding up the wooden stairs.   He opened the door and closed it quickly.   I jumped down from the window and ran across the room to him.

"I'm happy you are back," I purred as he picked me up. He smelled like fish. I licked his hand hungrily. He tasted like fish too!

"I brought you lunch," he said.

"*Grazie*, thank you," I meowed as I began to eat the delicate white fish he placed on the floor.

"Adriano? Adriano. Come back to the kitchen and help me with the dishes," a woman called.

"*Mia nonna*," he whispered. "She probably won't let me keep you, but let's go ask."

Adriano walked slowly. I jumped down each step without making a noise as I followed him., but Nonna saw me as we entered the kitchen. She screamed so loudly I jumped a meter straight up in the air. All of the fur on my tail puffed out and so did the fur on my back.

"Black cats are bad luck! Get that black cat out of this house *subito*, immediately!" she ordered Adriano in a nervous voice as she waved a wooden spoon in my direction and shooed me toward the door.

"You do not want that cat to curse your father's fishing business, do you?"

Adriano stepped between me and Nonna. He picked me up and walked slowly across the courtyard toward the gate.

"*Mi dispace*. I am sorry," he said sadly. "I like

you, *gattina*, but Nonna is superstitious, just like many of the people in Portazzurro." Adriano sighed as he patted my head. "You better find a different village away from the sea if you want a good home."

Adriano scratched behind my ear then dropped me over the gate. I heard his feet crunch on the sandy stone ground as he walked toward his house.

I laid down next to the gate, resting my head on my front paws. Making friends, especially with old people, was more complicated than I imagined. I had been so hopeful Adriano would be my new family, and hopeful I could live at the sea and eat fish every day, but I knew Adriano was right. I needed to find a different village.

I hopped up the stairs away from Adriano's house until I reached the last colorful building. "*I will miss Adriano and the giggling girls at the sea. I will miss sardines too,*" I thought, "*but I cannot stay in a village that does not like black cats.*"

I walked away from Portazzurro for many hours until the stars shone around the half-moon high above in the night sky.

Chapter 8
The Humming Lady

The next morning after eating two crickets and a fuzzy caterpillar, none of which tasted half as good as fresh fish, I walked past the road that led to Pudoia. This time, I followed the road and the stream toward *i monti*, the mountains.

I thought about each of the children I met at the sea. I could hear their laughter in my mind. "*I will find a good family,*" I thought, "*one with fun children!*"

I walked and walked.

The first day passed and then the second day. I wondered if I had made the right decision to come this way. Another day came and went. I did not see a single person, much less a village. A pit of loneliness grew inside me. It became heavier every day.

But I continued. What choice did I have? I was not welcome in Portazzurro and the city was too busy and loud for me. Only when I became exhausted did doubts loom over me like the thick blanket of clouds that hung in the sky. *"What if I don't find a family? What if I don't find the right family?"*

When Mother Cat had told me to be patient, I had not known it was going to take this long or be this hard to find the right family.

The sky drizzled rain, but I kept walking.

I curled up to sleep night after night with worrisome questions buzzing like bumblebees in my little head, but surprisingly, I slept peacefully. There were many good locations for me to sleep in the forest. I liked the tight spaces where the dirt and rocks were hollowed out of tree trunks the best. I felt safe, and I was never cold there.

The sixth night after leaving Portazzurro, the sky was finally clear again. I walked until very late with the full moon illuminating my path.

The next morning as I watched the sunrise, I

was filled with new hope. *"Maybe today will be the day I find my family."* Once again, I set out.

The mountain air was crisp and clean on my pink tongue. It smelled fresh and fragrant. I liked it. I also liked the music of the birds and the tall trees.

The trees were taller than anything I had ever seen before. They were even taller than the bell tower in Pudoia! I was very curious about being up that high. I chose the tallest tree and climbed.

From the treetop, I saw a long row of high rocky mountains, but better than that was seeing a small stone house with a smoking chimney in the distance. It was in a large field at the base of a green mountain.

"*Perfetto,*" I purred. "It is not a village, but perhaps the family who lives there is the perfect family for me!"

Eager to discover who lived in the house, I scurried down the tree. But as I walked, I thought about the many people who did not like me...the butcher's wife, the fish merchant, Adriano's grandmother. Would the people of this house feel the same way about me?

"*I should watch them before I introduce myself,*" I concluded. I knew I could approach the house without being seen or heard. "*Maybe I will be able to tell if they like black cats or not.*" I was excited to test my investigative plan. I walked faster.

The rocky road twisted right and left and went up and down many big hills as it followed the stream, but then strangely, the stream disappeared under a humongous white stone. I walked around the boulder, but there was no stream. *"That's odd! Where did it go?"* I wondered.

I searched for caterpillars to eat for breakfast, but I did not find any because it was a very cold morning, the coldest I had ever felt. Luckily, my fur, which had recently grown quite thick, kept me warm. Only the pads of my paws were cold because the ground was covered in delicate crystals. They crunched as I walked, and I left a trail of paw prints on the frosty ground.

I finally arrived at the little house late in the afternoon. Other than the chickens clucking in the yard, and a snoring brown goat, it was quiet.

"Where is the family?" I meowed. I walked around the outside of the fence looking for them. The window shutters were open, but the house was perfectly quiet. I looked up at the window, purred my short ascending tune, "Nrrr-uuu-mm-p," and jumped, landing on the narrow window sill.

A short bed was under the window with a shelf above. The shelf was full of books and colorful glass jars. Across the room, I saw a small table decorated with dried flowers in a dark green teardrop-shaped vase and a smoldering fire in the hearth.

Before I realized what I was doing, I jumped onto the bed and down to the wooden floor. The room smelled nice too. The scent of lavender filled my nose as a tall wooden barrel caught my eye. Always curious, I climbed up to the top of the barrel. To my great delight, it was full of *burro*, butter.

I happily licked the creamy, soft, salty *burro*, completely forgetting caution about the owners of the house who could return any minute.

"Cock a doodle doooo!" a rooster sang loudly.

The noise startled me, causing me to momentarily lose my balance. I stepped into the butter with one paw. As the rooster continued to crow every few seconds, I licked the butter from my paw. I do not like to have dirty paws.

"*I should go*," I thought. "*The sun is beginning to sink behind the mountain. Surely whoever lives here will return before it is dark.*" I jumped onto the bed. The colorful quilted blanket was soft and inviting. I was tempted to take a quick nap, but remembering how Adriano's *nonna* chased me out of her house with a wooden spoon, I decided it was safer to leave.

Outside again, this time with a full stomach, I looked for a place to watch for the owners of the house to return. On the other side of the yard near a garden there was a tree full of round orange fruits. "*I am small and black. It will be dark soon. I can hide among those fruits while I wait for the family to come home.*"

No sooner than I was high in the tree did my little ears twitch at the sound of faint music. Over several minutes the pleasant, but sad music gradually became more clear. Then a short woman with wavy black hair walked around the corner of the house. She carried a basket on one arm and held a long stick in her other hand.

"*Her hair is as black as the night sky before dawn, just like my fur!*" I thought, pleased we had something in common. As she walked into the yard, I noticed she was very, very old. "That's odd," I thought. "*All of the old people I've met have white hair.*"

"*Buona sera, polli,* good evening, chickens," she said. The rooster responded with a loud call. "*Buona sera,* Piero, my noisy rooster," she said as she squatted and reached her hands forward toward the chickens. "I brought you seeds from the forest." The chickens pecked at the seeds she scattered on the ground. The humming lady slowly rose and walked into the house.

"*Where is her family?*" I wondered. But no one followed her.

I sat in the tree a long time. Between my excellent night vision and the light of the full moon above, I could see well. I watched the humming lady unpack onions and mushrooms from her basket. She added small objects from her apron pocket to the colorful glass bottles on the shelf above her bed.

"What is she doing?" I meowed inquisitively.

I continued to watch her, fascinated. Next, she stacked several pieces of wood on the ashes in the hearth. She pointed her walking stick at them and stated, "*Incendiare,*" in a commanding voice.

Instantly, a fire with tall flames appeared. I watched her, amazed, as she warmed her hands at the blazing fire before she turned around. She stood looking at the table and two chairs.

"*Who sits in the other chair?*" I thought as I watched her wipe a tear from her wrinkled cheek. She sighed a heavy, long breath and then began to prepare food. When she reached for *il burro* to add to the large black pot hanging over the fire, she laughed.

"What in the world got into my butter today?" she said. She looked around the room. She smiled, shrugged her shoulders, and started humming a happy melody.

"*Oh good, she is not sad anymore.*" I did not want her to feel sad.

Meanwhile outside, the rooster was watching me in the tree. He strutted in circles around the base of the tree, crowing loudly after each lap.

"*I hope he cannot fly,*" I thought. But he could fly, or at least a little.

The rooster flapped his wings and lifted off the ground for a few seconds. Then, he tried again. After every attempt, he looked up at me with his small beady eyes. His sharp beak and long claws looked dangerous. I sat perfectly still, hoping to hide behind the orange fruits.

My stomach was beginning to cramp painfully from eating too much butter. I needed to get out of the tree soon. I moved stealthily to the back of the tree and began to climb down silently.

"Cock a doodle DOOO!" the rooster cried, loud enough to be heard for many kilometers.

"Piero! What is all the fuss?" the humming lady called through the window. "*Vieni*, come, I will give you more seeds if you will be quiet."

Fortunately for me, the rooster walked toward the house, giving me an excellent opportunity to escape. Before I darted silently across the little yard, I looked back at the house, the rooster held one wing awkwardly out from his side as he pecked at the seeds on the threshold of the little house.

"*I will find one of those nice mossy holes at the base of a tree to sleep in tonight, then I will watch the humming lady again tomorrow. I want to know more about her before I introduce myself. So far she seems nice, but I want to be certain.*"

I squeezed under the boards in the fence and walked across the field up into the woods where I chose the first hollowed tree trunk I saw.

The next morning, after a very peaceful sleep in a kitten-size opening at the base of a large tree, I crawled out and stretched my back into a high arch.

The air was much warmer than the previous day. I heard a rustling noise in the dry leaves behind me. "*I wish I had some pesce per colazione,*" I sighed. "*I am tired of eating insects and caterpillars.*"

I quietly walked around the tree and spied a green lizard. "*A lizard! Perfetto!*" Lizards are small, but they make as much noise as larger animals when they run through dry leaves. I easily tracked the lizard's movement under the leaves and caught it. It was not as tasty as fish, but it was much better than hairy caterpillars.

"*Hmmm, hmmm.*" I heard a faint beautiful song drifting on the morning breeze.

"*It's the humming lady!*"

I scampered into the dense brush next to my sleeping hole and waited. The humming lady approached unhurriedly, stopping frequently to pick up brown spiky balls.

"*Why does she want those?*" I wondered. She

passed without noticing me. Curious to see what she would do next, I followed her.   I watched her collect items from the forest and put them in her basket.

She added more spiky balls, one feather, which she seemed most delighted to find, pink flowers, and some orange mushrooms. Several times she spoke softly to the birds in the trees above. She called them each by name and mimicked their songs by whistling. Once as a lizard darted across the path in front of her, she giggled, reminding me of the girls at the sea.

When her basket was nearly full she turned around on the path and walked back the other way. Near the edge of the woods, she sat on a large white stone. She sighed. She looked sad or tired. I could not tell which.

"Ah, Stella, I am happy you and Tomasso fell in love, but I do miss you very much, my dear girl. My little house is too quiet now that you are away with your husband," she said mournfully.

She was sad again. A tear rolled down her nose and dropped onto her red apron. I wanted to greet her in my cheerful kitten way, but if she was

afraid of me, like so many other old people, I would only make her feel worse.

I watched her stand up and slowly walk across the field back to her house. Alone.

I wanted to make the right choice, the best choice. The humming lady was very different from the family I had imagined for so long. Could she be *la famiglia perfetta* Mother Cat said was waiting for me?

I caught another lizard and returned to the hole in the tree to think.

"*She's not young like Adriano, and she lives alone, not with children as I've always wanted,*" I reasoned, "*but I know she is friendly to animals from the way she talks to her chickens and the songbirds.*"

The longer I thought about the humming lady, the more confident I felt. Finally, I knew.

"*She will be kind to me,*" I concluded feeling good about my decision. "*Domani, tomorrow, I will introduce myself.*"

Chapter 9
Luna's Wonderful Surprise

"*Oggi è il giorno*, today is the day!" I purred happily as I woke up. "Today I choose the humming lady as my family." I crawled out of the hole in the tree and hastily completed my stretches.

Knowing the humming lady collected things in the woods and wanting desperately for her to find me, I sat near some orange mushrooms. "*If she likes me, she will take me home just as she does with her other forest treasures*," I thought. I tried to be patient, but it is very hard to be patient when you are waiting to meet your new family.

I heard a lizard in the leaves, but I left it alone and continued sitting politely with my tail wrapped around my front paws. "*What if she does not see me*," I fretted. I moved into the middle of the path and assumed my ladylike pose again.

My ears told me the humming lady was getting closer, but it felt like a long time before I saw her. She wore a red apron and carried a woven basket partially full of plants and those spiky balls.

"*Allora*, gracious goodness! How did you get to Speranzamonte, Hope Mountain?" she exclaimed. "*Buongiorno, io sono Luna*, good morning, I am Luna," she said as she knelt in the middle of the path.

"*Luna*," I repeated to myself. "*Just like the moon. What a lovely name.*"

"I did not expect to find you, *una dolce gattina nera*, a sweet black kitten on my walk today. You are a wonderful surprise!" Luna marveled. I cocked my head to the side as I listened.

"Where are you from? I have lived here for many moons, but I have not seen a cat in these woods since I was a young girl, back in the days of the fairies."

I cocked my head to the other side. I was relieved she was happy to see me. Then forgetting Mother Cat's warnings, I stood up and stretched my back into a high arch. I was stiff from sitting still. Luna calmly watched me, then she reached her hand forward.

"*Fantastico! She's not afraid of me!*" I thought.

I sniffed her hand. She smelled like butter and lavender.

She patted the top of my head and smiled. "*Sei bellissima,* you are very beautiful. I like your black fur. We have black hair in common, don't we, little one?" she said with a wink. She stroked me softly from my head to the tip of my tail.

My heart swelled with happiness at her touch. I purred loudly, leaning forward into her hand. Her hand was much smaller than the kind butcher's hand, and her skin was much softer than young Adriano's skin. I instantly felt relaxed.

"Grrrrrrr!" My stomach growled.

"*Basta*! Stop, stop!" I meowed. Embarrassed, I hung my head down and stared at my paws.

"*Allora gattina*, you are hungry. It is not good for a kitten to be hungry. *Vieni*, come. Come with me to my humble home. I will share good food and rich goat's milk with you. You may stay as long as you like." Luna smiled as she gently picked me up.

"Do not be afraid, *mia piccola gatta nera*," she said as she put me in her apron pocket.

My heart swelled with happiness again. Luna had called me *her* cat.

"You are in luck, *gattina*. Early this morning I made my best recipe; roasted chicken! My noisy rooster, Piero, broke his wing trying to get into my persimmon tree last night. I am grateful now for his accident because I have the perfect breakfast for you!" Luna smiled brightly.

After a week of travel, riding in Luna's apron was a welcome treat. If I sat up, I could see over the edge of her pocket, but the slow rhythm of her walking and her soothing voice soon made me feel sleepy.

"I'm happy you are comfortable, little one," she said as she reached in and patted the top of my head. "Only a short while longer and we will be home."

"*Home*," I purred.

"I am happy to have a guest. My great-niece, Stella, married and moved away last year. I miss her terribly. I hope to visit her in *Venezia*, Venice at Christmas…if the weather is nice. Travel is challenging at my age," Luna mused with a quiet laugh.

She stopped once to pick pink flowers and their heart-shaped leaves. "See how the flower petals turn upward? Cyclamen are my favorite flowers. And the leaves are an essential ingredient in an old

family potion I make to cure heartburn."

Luna seemed happy to have a new friend. She talked and talked. I enjoyed listening. She had a pleasant voice and she was very interesting.

"I know how to make lots of special recipes," she continued. "I will show you my collection of books and potion bottles when we get home."

"*So that is what all of the colored bottles on the shelf are,*" I thought.

As we passed a steep, rocky trail, Luna told me about her olive grove at the end of the path. "I just finished bottling this season's *olio d'olivia*, olive oil.

My olive oil is the best oil this side of Venice," she said proudly. "It is also the secret to my excellent health and my youthful hair."

I did not want to miss anything Luna said. She was so interesting, but I was getting sleepy. I yawned.

"Are you tired?" Luna asked, pausing to catch her breath. "Did you have a long journey? I am so glad I found you before a hungry fox ate you for dinner. I will have to tell you all about the saint from Assisi. He is a protector of animals. One of my great-grandmothers met Saint Francis once."

"The man at the fountain in Pudoia told me about him!" I meowed, but of course, Luna did not understand me.

She scratched the top of my head. "I am grateful to have a new friend. We are both fortunate today, aren't we? I think I will call you Fortuna. Do you like your name, *mia piccola gatta nera?*"

"*Sì, sì, sì,*" I purred in agreement, feeling very proud to have a name. If this was what having a human family was like, I had made an excellent choice.

Chapter 10
Life with Luna

I followed Luna everywhere, listening and learning. I adapted easily to her routine of rising early, eating frequent small meals, and taking long walks in the woods. When Luna worked in her garden, I hunted bugs, not because I was hungry, but because it was fun.

I liked being with Luna. She was calm and quiet. Her gentle touches made me feel happy. She was also the most interesting human I had ever met. Listening to Luna I learned the names and songs of many birds. Luna could whistle their songs almost as well as the birds themselves!

She also talked frequently about the plants she

used for cooking and the special ingredients she collected for her concoctions. She answered many of my questions about the woods as if she could read my mind. I even learned why the stream I followed out of Pudoia disappeared into the mountainside. She said the water from high in the Dolomite Mountains often flows underground for long distances before it rises to the surface again. Life with Luna was fascinating.

Luna seemed to be fascinated with me too. I often saw her pause from her work or her reading to watch me. She always smiled as she watched me play. I felt good knowing I made Luna happy.

One morning after a walk to collect the brown spiky balls Luna called chestnuts, she said, "*Vieni*, come, Fortuna and I will tell you about my mother."

"Nrrr-uuu-mm-p," I sang as I jumped onto her lap. Stories were one of my favorite parts of living with Luna.

"When I was five or six years old, my mother started my formal education. She had always read to me, but she began to teach me to read." Luna paused and pointed her crooked finger toward her collection of books. "She said reading would open the world to me, even if I never traveled far away from home."

"I wish I could share stories about my mother and brothers with Luna," I thought.

Luna continued, "I did not understand at the time, but she was nurturing my imagination and my knowledge. I know now both of these things have helped me live a long and rich life. You see, Fortuna, even though magical abilities come easily to my family, she taught me, creativity and study are required to think of possibilities never thought of before. Most magic is simply science that cannot be explained yet."

"What is science?" I wondered. I knew what magic was because I saw how Luna started the fire each night.

"Mother told me stories about fantastical creatures and far away lands where people did impossible things such as travel to the moon. She also read lessons and recipes to me from our spell books, and she made me practice before I could play outside."

"The first spell I learned is used for moving objects without touching them. '*Movento spotstari.*' I practiced saying that for hours and hours until I mastered moving pebbles, then acorns, and later ripe olives. Eventually, I learned to move bigger and heavier objects such as stones, but that is very exhausting, so I do not do it often."

"*Wow!*" I thought imagining stones moving through the air. "*I hope I get to see Luna do more magic!*"

"I still use this spell every autumn when I harvest my olives. I shake the tree trunks so the branches drop all of the ripe olives into my baskets. You will see next harvest how well this technique works. It is especially helpful now that I cannot climb trees anymore. Years ago, I was quite a good climber, but not as good as you are, Fortuna. You are an excellent climber now that you are healthy and strong from eating my good cooking."

I sat up and touched my moist black nose to Luna's chin as a thank you for the compliment.

"*Allora*, you have grown! You will always be a small cat, but do not worry. Being petite never stopped me from doing anything. And your fur is so shiny now. My olive oil does wonders for your fur just like it does for my hair." Luna tossed her hair over her shoulder playfully.

I did feel stronger. Luna was also right about her good cooking. She was an even better cook than she was a storyteller.

Meats were my favorite foods she made, but we did not eat them daily. Luna picked persimmons and baked fresh bread for breakfast. I liked the bread soaked in milk from the goat, Capra. Luna usually ate vegetables for *pranzo*, lunch, while I enjoyed eggs and on occasion stewed tomatoes, but my favorite food was Luna's roasted chicken.

The meat was juicy and delicious with just the perfect blend of spices and *sale*, salt. The smell was almost as wonderful as the taste! My nose learned to tell exactly when the meat was most tender. I meowed to alert Luna and she always laughed, saying, "Why I think you are right, it is perfectly cooked now."

Luna interrupted my thoughts about roasted chicken by saying, "I am feeling energetic today. V*ieni*, let's go for another walk. I want to show you my special olive trees. They are all grafted from one tree which I call Luigi."

"*Luna has a name for everything,*" I thought. "*She truly is a friend to her animals and nature too.*"

"I hope you do not get tired on the steep path because you are too big now to fit into my apron pocket." Luna giggled. She laughed a lot these days.

I did not feel tired. I had lots of energy, and I was excited to explore a new place. I walked ahead of Luna so I could hear lizards before her footsteps scared them away. "*Someday maybe I can teach her to walk quietly like a black cat does best,*" I thought.

Luna had to stop and rest several times while we climbed the steep, rocky path to the olive grove. Each time, I trotted back to her, not wanting her to be alone. She picked up a white stone and turned it in her hand. "Dolomite mineral makes this stone white. These stones are what makes the mountain strong," she said looking up.

"*I wonder if I will ever know as much as Luna?*" I thought as we continued walking.

While Luna inspected the olive trees, I climbed them. I love climbing to high places. From the top of Luigi, I could see all the way to the sea!

"It is a glorious day, little one," Luna said while leaning on her walking staff as she caught her breath. "Can you see *Venezia*, Venice today?"

"*Sì*," I meowed.

Luna looked up at me. "Stella climbed these trees when she was a young girl. I miss her, but thanks to you, I am not lonely anymore."

I climbed down to a lower branch and leaned forward touching my nose to Luna's chin.

"*Grazie*, Fortuna. What a blessing you are to me. I found you when I needed a friend the most. I am grateful you decided to stay with me."

That afternoon Luna and I napped together. I woke first because cats like to take short naps, but Luna was tired from our hike. She snored softly. I stepped over her without waking her.

Luna's basket of smooth brown chestnuts was on the table. This morning before she brought them in the house, she peeled off the spiky parts and threw them in the garden. She said it added nutrients to the soil. I do not know what nutrients are, but I knew playing with the nuts would be fun. I could not resist them any longer!

"*I'll just take one out and play with it quietly so I will not wake Luna,*" I thought. I cupped my left paw and

scooped a nut from the top of the basket.

It flew through the air and made a delightful clacking noise as it bounced on the floor.

"*This is even more fun than I imagined*," I thought, immediately forgetting to play quietly. I scooped out another chestnut, sending it sailing high before it landed and bounced across the floor.

Click, clack, clack, clack....

In no time, Luna's basket was half full and I was having a marvelous time!

"*Now what?*" I thought.

"*I will pretend they are lizards and practice my hunting skills.*" I crouched low on the table, wiggled my hips, and pounced down onto a chestnut. I kicked it with my left paw and chased it across the room, batting it again in the other direction with my right paw. I was so focused on my game, I did not hear the bed creak as Luna woke from her nap.

"You certainly are enjoying yourself, aren't you, little one?" she asked.

I looked up at Luna, nervous she might be upset I emptied her basket and woke her from a nap, but she was smiling.

"Watching you play makes me smile, but we need to clean up. Christmas will be here soon. I always roast chestnuts in the fire on Christmas Eve as I celebrate the birth of our Savior King."

Fortunately for Luna, she had already collected chestnuts, because a few days later, the temperatures dropped sharply, the sky became cloudy, and we woke to find a thick white blanket covering Speranzamonte.

"*Neve*, snow!" Luna exclaimed. "We will stay home for Christmas this year, little one. I am too old to travel in slippery weather."

Chapter 11

Epiphany

"*Stanotte*, tonight is a very special night. It is Epiphany, the twelfth night after Christmas. Tonight we celebrate the visit of the kings, also known as magi, to baby Jesus. The magi traveled by following a bright star to deliver gifts to Jesus. In my family, this holiday has an extra special meaning. You see Fortuna, the magi stopped to rest at the house of my great-great-great grandmother, Befana, on their way to find the holy family.

"*It must be nice to have kings visit. I think that would be exciting! I wonder what they looked like?*" I thought.

"Before they left Befana's house, they invited her to join them on their journey, but she felt she was too busy with her chores to go. She did not accept their invitation. Later that night, she regretted her decision. She set out from her house to find the kind kings, but she did not find them," Luna explained.

"*How sad for Befana,*" I thought. "*I would have gone with them. I like adventures and following friends.*"

"Ever since that night long long ago, Befana has delivered gifts to children in honor of the gifts the magi gave Jesus. I have not seen Befana since I was a girl, but I have many wonderful memories, and of course, I inherited her books."

Luna rose from her chair and lifted a big, brown leather book from the shelf. I smelled it. It smelled old and musty, causing me to sneeze daintily.

"*Salute,* health, Fortuna," Luna said. "Did you know of all of the silly superstitions Italians have about black cats, they think it is good luck to hear a black cat sneeze? People are funny, don't you agree?"

I walked across the book and looked up at Luna agreeing with her that people have many ridiculous beliefs about black cats.

"We must be careful with my books, Fortuna. They are very old, even older than I am! These books contain knowledge about this land, stories of my family, wonderful recipes, and many secrets."

"Meow," I responded.

"Fortuna, sometimes I think you understand what I'm saying. You are quite smart, aren't you?"

"Meow!"

"*I do understand!*" I thought. I made eye contact with Luna. She had a twinkle in her eyes which meant she had a new idea.

"I wonder," Luna said. She touched her crooked index finger to her lips, concentrating on her idea. "If I could make a concoction that would give you the gift of speech? I have a feeling you have a lot to say."

I jumped off the table, onto the bed, and up to the shelf with the rest of Luna's books. "Which book do you need, Luna?" I meowed.

Luna giggled. She walked across the room slowly. "Patience, Fortuna, new magic takes time," she said. "I will start studying *domani*. Hopefully, I will succeed, but it may take a long time. I've never known a speaking cat before, but hard work, especially here on Speranzamonte, makes many things possible!"

"*Grazie*," I purred to Luna.

"*When Luna succeeds, I will be able to tell her my own story. I can't wait to tell her about Mother Cat, my brothers, the kind butcher, the awful butcher's wife, my trip to the sea....*"

My mind raced with excitement. "*What fun I will have telling Luna my story.*"

Chapter 12

The Boy

"*Buongiorno*," I rehearsed in my head how I would greet Luna. I stretched my back and sat up in bed. *"I hope today is the day she finishes the potion so I can tell her my story."* Two and a half months had passed since Luna's idea on Epiphany night. She was entertained with her daily reading, but I was bored. If only Luna had a family who lived with her. I liked living with Luna, but sometimes I still wished I had found a family with children.

As Luna softly snored I silently crept outside. Capra, the goat, was still sleeping too. *"I am ready to play and have an adventure, not sleep!"* I thought as I stretched again.

I set out across the yard and jumped over the gate in one swift leap. *"Now what?"* I asked myself. I was in the mood for something fun. I sat on a large stone in Luna's field thinking. *"Maybe I'll think of an idea if I can see more. I'll go to my favorite lookout tree in Luna's olive grove."*

The predawn sky did not slow me down because cats see very well in the dark. I scampered up the steep, rocky path and climbed a tree, just in time to watch the sunrise. The sky woke up behind the rocky snow-covered mountains in the east making the land beyond appear out of the darkness.

As the morning light cast a pink glow across the sky, I heard a faint high-pitched whistling followed by animal sounds. The animal noises were not low bellowing sounds like the big brown and white animals I saw months ago, but a different sound, one I had never heard before.

"Perfetto! Now I have an adventure for the day — I am going to find out what animal that is."

I climbed down the trunk of the old olive tree, leaped over the low white stone wall, and ran down the rocky path. The chimney was not smoking and

the shutters were not open yet as I passed Luna's house. My ears twitched with excitement as I followed the mysterious sounds away from Luna's yard.

As the chorus of shrill whistles and bleating noises grew, I heard human voices too. *"Bene!"* I thought. *"New friends! Luna has not had any olive oil customers in a long time. I miss making new friends."*

When I rounded the next corner, I saw the

road end at a field. A large herd of fluffy white animals with skinny legs and long ears covered half of the field. I knew from Luna's stories they were *pecore*, sheep.

I saw big, fat sheep with curved horns, skinny sheep, and more small sheep that skipped and scampered than I could count. The lambs made frequent sudden jumps in attempts to stay in rhythm with the big sheep who walked in a large, white wobbly mass in front of their shepherd. The shepherd had a long grey beard. He wore a green coat and matching green felt hat adorned with a long, brown hawk's feather.

"The lambs are playful like I am," I thought. *"I can hardly wait to play with them!"*

I started toward the lambs at the front of the herd, but then I saw a better playmate, a boy! He walked on the far side of the herd whistling and waving his arm in a forward sweeping motion to guide the animals. *"This is going to be the best day! A boy! A boy to play with me!"* Before I finished my thought, I was running top speed down the road to meet my new friend.

I reached the field quickly. The grass was damp with morning dew and higher than I expected, making it impossible to continue running fast.

"Jump as you did at the beach," I thought. I did not want to waste a minute of playtime with the boy.

"Fweeeet, fweeeet-t-t-t!" the boy whistled, urging the sheep forward.

The sheep did not listen. They stood still eating grass, ignoring the boy. They must have been extremely hungry because they ignored me too as I jumped past them through the middle of the herd.

"Andiamo, pecore. Let's go, sheep!" The shepherd called from the back of the herd.

"FWEEEET!! FWEEEEEEET-T-T-T-T!!!"

The shepherd's whistle was much louder and longer than the boy's whistle. It startled the sheep. Two lambs close to me jumped straight in the air at the piercing sound. The big sheep bleated, then obediently walked forward.

"I am in big trouble!" I realized suddenly as the entire herd of sheep began to walk at a hurried pace. Even the lambs towered over me. I could not hear or see the boy anymore as the hard hooves of the sheep

stamped the ground.

"Meow, meow!" I cried in fright, but my voice was no match for the noisy herd. I tried to move with the sheep. *"I am fast. Maybe I can get ahead of the herd and get to the boy."* I ran and jumped through the grass, but I was not big enough to keep up.

The sheep did not move in straight lines like Mother Cat taught me and my brothers to walk. They alternatively walked and ran, moving right and left, bumping one another and bumping me.

"Meowwwww!" I cried in pain as a lamb stepped on my tail.

I could not see anything except hooves, legs, and tails. *"Why didn't I wait on the side of the road for the boy?"* I scolded myself as the shadow of a sheep moved over me like a large, thick rain cloud.

A sharp pain shot through my head. The beautiful bright morning instantly became dark.

Chapter 13
The Shepherd and His Wife

I was dizzy when I woke. I felt like I was floating. I hurt so much, especially my head, I could not open my eyes. The only movement I managed was to twitch the tip of my tail.

"*Piccola gatta,* what were you doing in the middle of a field of *pecore*?" a gentle voice asked.

I still heard sheep and the whistle of the boy, but not the loud shrill whistle of the shepherd. "*I think the shepherd is carrying me,*" I reasoned.

"*Mia moglie,* my wife, will know what to do for you. Be brave," the shepherd said, reassuring me. "We are almost home to Maria."

"*Home?*" I thought. "*I have a home! I chose Luna. Where is Luna?*" I thought anxiously.

My tail twitched faster. Not only was I badly hurt, but my disappearance would hurt Luna. She would be lonely and sad again without me.

My head throbbed, and I fainted....

"Maria! Maria, come quickly, *presto*!"

"*Caro*, dear Lorenzo, what do you have in your hat this time? Another injured animal? A bird perhaps?" Maria asked.

"The sheep trampled a kitten. She needs your healing touch," Lorenzo answered.

"Bring her inside and I will see what I can do. You and Giovanni come in for *pranzo*, lunch while *il pane e la zuppa*, the bread and soup, are hot.

Lorenzo passed me to his wife. She carried me inside where I smelled fresh bread and strong cheese. My whole body hurt as she lifted me out of Lorenzo's hat. "Meow, meow," I cried still unable to open my eyes because of the intense pain.

"*Shhhhh*, I know you must hurt, *gattina*, but let me clean you, and bandage your injuries, then you can sleep as long as you need," Maria said softly.

Maria was gentle. She worked efficiently as if she was experienced caring for injured animals. In a matter of minutes, my fur was clean. She wrapped cloth around my head and placed me on a blanket next to the warm hearth.

"Try to sleep, *gattina*. I will check on you soon. I think with time, you will heal. You are lucky you are a cat! Cats are capable of amazing recoveries." I felt Maria's hand on my side. She muttered something under her breath I could not understand before she stepped away.

I don't remember anything else from that day or much from the next few days. I slept most of the time. When I woke, my head pulsed with pain and there seemed to be two of every object in the shepherd's house, even the shepherd and his wife.

Days passed into nights and back into days several times before my eyes stopped doubling everything, but my vision remained blurry. Since I could not see clearly, I relied on my other senses. Mostly I listened. The sheep baaed to each other constantly, but they were most excited when Lorenzo greeted them at dawn and when Giovanni visited in the afternoon. I wished I was not hurt so I could run and play outside with Giovanni. I heard him play with the lambs upon his arrival each afternoon, but when Maria called him inside, he sat and read silently until dinner.

"I wish he would read stories out loud to me," I thought longingly. *"I miss Luna's stories, and I miss our walks, and being outside,"* I was sad not knowing when, or if, I would ever feel like a playful, energetic young cat again.

More days passed with the same dull routine. My head and my eyes were slowly healing, but I still had headaches. As the days grew longer, Lorenzo spent longer hours outside. Maria mostly stayed inside cooking, cleaning, and making cheese. The cheese smelled funny, but it tasted wonderful.

Maria gave me small saucers of fresh milk and spoonfuls of ricotta cheese several times a day. At first, she placed the food next to my blanket by the hearth, but she gradually moved it further from my blanket. Every time I stood, the room seemed to tilt and shift. I struggled to walk a few steps to the bowl, but I did it.

One morning, weeks after my accident, Maria placed my food bowl halfway across the room. She knelt next to the bowl of ricotta cheese and encouraged me as I stood and stretched.

"Come, eat, so you will regain your strength. You can do it, *gattina,*" she coaxed me.

"*Bene, bene,* good!" She praised me with a gentle pat as I finally reached the bowl. I was too tired to walk back to the blanket after I ate. I lay down on the floor. When I woke, a bright square of sunlight shone through the window onto the floor around me.

The warmth of the light on my black fur was delightful. It was a different kind of warmth than the heat of a fire. It was an energizing heat. For the first time since I got hurt, I felt like a tiny bit like a kitten again. I sat up, wrapping my tail around my front paws, and turned my face toward the light.

"You know, *mia nonna* always said cats have seven lives. In some places, people say cats have as many as nine lives. I don't know about all of that. I think it's probably just an old wives' tale, but seeing how well you are improving, I believe you have a long life ahead of you, *gattina*. I am certain you will be strong enough to play outside soon."

I repeated her encouraging words in my head as I enjoyed the sunshine. She thought I was getting better. My pain was improving, even if my eyes did not work well yet. "*If Maria is right, I will feel like myself again…one day. As soon as I have the strength, I am going to home to Luna!*"

With each new day, I missed Luna more and more. I found myself thinking about her all day, and also at night when I could not sleep. "*If I could just get back to Luna. I don't care anymore if she is old and tired and cannot play with me. I just want to be with her.*"

Maria continued placing my food bowl further away until one day it sat waiting for me in the open doorway. After walking from the city to the sea and then to the mountains, I could not believe how tired I felt walking across one small room, but I made it. Maria was right; I was improving, but I was impatient and bored.

After I ate, I sat on the threshold and looked out into the yard. I could hear the sheep, but I could not see them because their pen was around the corner of the house. I could not see the mountain either, but I knew from the position of the sun that it was behind the house.

"*How will I get back to Luna? I know which direction to go, but I don't know how far away she is. I am too weak to try today, but I will try soon to walk home!*" I lay down on the blanket and closed my eyes, picturing home and my best friend. "*I wish I had some of Luna's magical powers so I could go home right this minute,*" I thought. "*Wouldn't Luna be surprised to see me appear at her garden gate?*"

"It is a beautiful, warm spring morning, a perfect day for the first market of the season. I am going with Lorenzo to sell cheese. *Ciao, gattina.* We will be back before dark," Maria said cheerfully as she crossed the yard."

"*The market!*" I repeated to myself excitedly, "*Luna has told me she goes to the market to sell her olive oil when the weather is nice. I have to go to the market today!*"

"Meow, meow," I said following Maria. But despite my attempt to plead with her, they rode away on the wagon pulled by a donkey.

"*If only Luna had already perfected the concoction, I*

could tell them I belong with Luna!" I thought.

Now I was alone. I missed Luna more than ever. Luna was not who I imagined as my family when I left Mother Cat; she was even better! When I was with Luna, I never felt sad or lonely like I did now. I shut my eyes tight and thought about how good I felt when Luna used to hold me in her lap.

"*Luna loves me*," I realized. "*And I love her too.*"

"*As soon as I can, I am coming home to you, Luna,*" I meowed in the direction of the mountain. With hopeful and determined thoughts, I drifted into a peaceful nap.

Hours later I woke, hearing the distant sound of wagon wheels crunching across the rocky road. I opened my eyes. The yard looked blurry, but then I realized it was wet. The air was thick with moisture. As I listened to the wagon approach, a big cloud moved and an arch of colors appeared in the sky.

"How beautiful," I meowed, looking at the colors. I was marveling at the rainbow when my ears twitched, hearing a pleasant, familiar sound. I strained to listen. "*Am I dreaming?*"

The noise of the wagon grew louder. The

lambs began to run and jump in the pen, knowing their shepherd was coming home. Between the chorus of happily bleating sheep, my ears heard humming music.

Feeling like my dreams were coming true, I ran across the yard to the wagon.

"Luna! Luna! Luna!" I meowed. There she was, sitting in the wagon to Maria's right, my Luna! Luna stopped humming when she saw me. She put her hands on her chest and smiled. Her eyes glistened with tears as she looked at me.

Luna climbed down from the wagon faster than I had ever seen her move before. She knelt in the road and I climbed into her lap. She drew me into a tight embrace. I purred so loudly my whole body vibrated. Nothing hurt.

Luna embraced me for a long time as tears rolled down her cheeks onto the top of my head.

"Fortuna, my Fortuna, I am overwhelmed with joy! I prayed for you daily, *mia piccola gatta nera*. I hoped and prayed for your safety and your return home. This morning God answered my prayers through this good shepherd and his wife."

Luna told me how she asked everyone at the market if they had seen a small black cat. When she asked Lorenzo, he smiled and said, "*Allora*, so that is where she came from!"

"Luna," Maria said. "will you please join us for *cena*, dinner?"

"*Grazie.* You are very generous, Maria, but I am ready to take Fortuna home," Luna answered as she smiled at me. Her eyes were still moist with her tears, but she was happy.

"Are you ready to go home?" she asked me.

"Meow, meow," I answered lovingly.

Maria held me while Lorenzo helped Luna up into the wagon. I licked her hands. These were the hands that cared for me while I was hurt. She returned my loving gesture with a kiss on the top of my head. "I will visit you soon, Fortuna. I will bring you fresh ricotta cheese," Maria said, smiling sweetly as she passed me to Luna.

"*This must be what true happiness is,*" I thought, sitting in Luna's lap as we bounced along the road in Lorenzo's wagon. I did not even mind how the bumps in the road made my headache worse. I was perfectly content to be with Luna.

Luna hummed happily the entire ride home.

Chapter 14
Home

"*Benvenuta a casa*, welcome home," Luna said to me with a wide smile as the donkey stopped in front of the garden gate. The garden was already full of tall tomato plants growing generously with Luna's expert and magical care.

"*Grazie*, thank you, kind Lorenzo, for saving Fortuna. Please wait while I get a bottle of my olive oil for you as *un regalo piccolo*, a small gift."

Luna sat me on the wagon seat next to Lorenzo. After a few minutes, she returned with a large green jug of olive oil. Seeing her struggle with the weight of the bottle, Lorenzo stepped down from the wagon and took the bottle from her.

"*Grazie* Luna. I hear your olive oil is the best

olio d'oliva this side of *Venezia.*"

"*Grazie,* Signore Lorenzo," Luna said modestly. "Tell Maria, drinking two spoonfuls of my olive oil every day will be good for her health, and her hair."

"*Arrivederci,* good bye, Signora Luna."

"*Arrivederci e grazie,* Signore Lorenzo," replied Luna as she carefully picked me up from the wagon seat and carried me inside.

"*Home. I am home,*" I thought joyfully.

Luna made my favorite recipe, roasted chicken, for my homecoming dinner celebration. I sat on the table so I could be close to Luna. While the chicken was cooking, she opened a bottle of wine from the top shelf. "Good food and good wine are best enjoyed with a good story. I will tell you about my work while you were gone."

"*Fantastico,*" I thought.

"But first, I want you to try this," Luna said as she lifted a small turquoise blue bottle the color of the Italian sea from her shelf. "It will help you heal faster, though Maria says you are making miraculous progress on your own. It tastes sour, but it works wonders on my many aches and pains."

Luna was right. The liquid was sour, but I licked it anyway.

"I did not know what happened to you or why you did not return. I was sad, worried, and lonely," Luna began. "The first few days you were gone, I searched everywhere for you. I walked all of the trails in the woods, up to the olive grove, and along the stream, but there was no sign of you because you were kilometers away at the shepherd's house. My loneliness exhausted me more than a walk up to the olive grove in the summer heat. I did my chores and cooked for myself, but I thought about you all day long and most of the night too."

"I worried a wild animal had hurt you or that you were lost. I prayed for God to protect you and bring you home. I did not know for sure you would come back to me, but I remained hopeful you would, so I doubled my efforts on perfecting the speaking concoction. I gathered fresh spring ingredients to test in the potion all the while praying for you."

I purred loudly, grateful to be with Luna.

"Yesterday as I was praying for you, an idea

popped into my mind. I knew I needed to add fairy dust to the concoction. Fairy dust is a key ingredient in many of my potions. When I did, it shimmered like diamonds as a completed potion always does! But sadly, the shimmer faded quickly. After a few seconds, it was dull and cloudy again."

Luna held up a yellow bottle with a picture of a black cat on it. The contents looked like milk.

"*Allora, mia gatta nera*, I am sorry. I have not completed my promise to you. I tried. I do not have any more fairy dust and that is exactly what the potion needs," Luna said looking disappointed.

I rubbed my cheek against Luna. She scratched behind my ear in my favorite spot. "*Vieni*, Fortuna. Come sit with me. I'll tell you a story. We have both had an exciting day. I need to rest."
Luna sat in her chair. I turned once in a circle, and curled up, perfectly content in her lap. I did not even feel sad Luna's potion had failed.

"When I was about six years old my mother taught me how to use flower petals to collect fairy dust," Luna began. "Most people imagine fairies live high in the trees because they can fly, but they actually prefer to live in the bases of old tree trunks in the soft mossy hollowed-out part."

My ears twitched as I thought of the forest.

"Low to the ground, fairies are protected from the wind and most birds," she continued.

As Luna further described fairy houses, I realized I had slept in a fairy house in the woods close to her house the two nights before we first met. I sat up and looked directly at Luna.

"Mother taught me the location of the fairy houses in these woods. Because I was small and nimble. I could easily crouch low to reach into the tight spaces under the trees."

"*I am smaller and more flexible than a child,*" I thought. "*I even fit inside the fairy house I found!*"

"Meow!" I said excitedly.

"As a child, I spent hours in the woods searching for fairies. Fairies are very shy, but I knew where to look."

"Meow, meow, meow," I interrupted, wishing Luna could read my thoughts.

"I wish I had more fairy dust, Fortuna, but before I knew that was what I needed, I used it to fertilize the garden."

I jumped down from Luna's lap and trotted to the door. "Meow," I called as if to say 'follow me!'

"What is it, *mia piccola gatta nera?*" Luna asked. "Do you need to go outside?" Luna rose slowly and opened the door.

I ran halfway across the garden toward the gate, energized by my revelation.

"Meow!" I repeated, impatiently.

"*Allora*, Fortuna. I am coming. Let me get my walking stick and my basket."

I led Luna through the field, up the hillside, and into the woods. I walked ahead on the path. She followed as quickly as she was able. When we reached the place where we first met, I stepped off the path into the brush.

"*Dove stiamo andando?* Where are we going?" Luna asked, perplexed.

I circled the tree trunk. I was now convinced it was a fairy house. Luna carefully stepped off the path. She gasped and patted her chest with one hand when she saw the base of the tree.

"Fortuna, you do understand me! You have

led me to a fairy house I've never seen before. Perhaps fairies still do live in these woods! I can hardly believe my eyes."

I crouched low to the ground and crawled into the opening in the tree trunk. It was just as I remembered. It was cozy, warm, and full of squishy green moss. I did not see any fairies or any fairy dust, but when I emerged, Luna gasped again.

"Fortuna! You've done it! The top of your head, the fur on your back, and your tail are covered in fairy dust!"

I looked up at Luna. She smiled back at me with a youthful twinkle in her dark eyes. Luna carried me home in her basket. She walked faster than normal.

As I stood on the table, Luna rubbed a red poppy flower petal over my fur. I stood very still so we did not waste any of the magical ingredient. Luna folded the petal into a cone and carefully poured the dust into the empty pink bottle with a fairy picture on the front.

She did not say anything, which was unusual. I was quiet too, excited and nervous about what would happen next.

Next, Luna meticulously added fairy dust to the milky potion in the yellow bottle. Immediately, it sparkled brightly as if she had added fireflies. She smiled.

"Are you ready?" she asked.

"Meow," I eagerly answered.

Luna poured the thick sparkling liquid onto a silver spoon and held it in front of me.

I licked the potion. Initially, it tasted bitter, but then the taste transformed in my mouth. It tasted like wild honey and freshly fallen snow. My mouth buzzed and tingled as Luna's potion touched the back of my tongue and my throat. My throat became very warm, almost hot, as I swallowed, but disappointingly the rest of my body felt exactly the same as before.

"Oh no, Luna, it did not work."

Luna laughed and picked me up. She twirled around like the young girls at the sea before she said, "Fortuna, *mia piccola gatta nera*, it did work! You just spoke seven words!"

I looked up at Luna with wide eyes. I was so

used to having conversations with her in my head, I did not realize my thoughts became words she could hear and understand. I was overjoyed.

I could speak!

"It did work, Luna! You are amazing! *Grazie mille!* I have so much to tell you," I said rapidly.

"I am sure you do, Fortuna! I want to hear everything. Come and sit with me. Tonight you are the storyteller."

Luna and I stayed up very late that first night I was back home. We were delighted with my new ability. I told Luna about life in the city with Mother Cat and my travels to the sea. She listened without interrupting me.

In the weeks and months that followed, Luna and I were inseparable. We were both so happy to be together again. When my head hurt, or my vision was blurry, I was able to tell Luna. She gave me healing remedies from her books. Every day I felt better until one day I chased a small yellow butterfly through the garden and high up into the persimmon tree without losing my balance. I finally felt like myself again.

We resumed our routine of rising early and going for walks to gather Luna's ingredients for cooking and potions. We talked morning, noon, and night.

Luna asked me many questions. She said she was curious about my experiences and perspectives because she had never talked to a cat before. I answered the best I could. I felt very proud teaching wise Luna.

With much practice, on her part, I even taught her how to walk quietly in the woods as a black cat does best.

"I wish I had known how to walk quietly like a black cat as a young girl," she said. "I probably scared most of the fairies deep into the woods with loud footsteps and girlish singing."

"Now we can look for them together, Luna. I think we will find many."

"Perhaps you are correct, Fortuna. After all of these years, I would love to see a fairy again."

"Luna, how did you know I would come back?" I asked.

"Life is uncertain. Even with all of my years

of experience and studying, I do not know the future, but I never gave up hope of your return. I knew you were a survivor. I knew you had traveled a long way to this mountain, and I knew you came to me at my most lonely time. I just had to trust that you were okay."

"I thought about you too, Luna…all of the time. I am glad my story of finding a family has a happy ending with you."

"*Anch'io*, me too, Fortuna."

I purred and touched my nose to her cheek.

Epilogue: The Birthday Gift

Many moons have passed since I first spoke. Luna and I have celebrated numerous holidays together and worked to expand her olive oil business. We have hosted Lorenzo, Maria, and Giovanni for dinners, and Luna built a bigger house to make room for guests and Stella's growing family. She and Tomasso have two boys now. We both love having visitors, but I rarely talk except when I am alone with Luna.

Luna and I lead a quiet, simple life. She works in her garden daily, and I check on the olive trees since the hike is hard for her. At night we take turns telling stories. After years of practice, I am a good storyteller too, although I cannot change my voice for different characters as easily as Luna can.

My favorite story to share is still my own. Every year on my birthday I retell my story. Today, I am eight years old. Luna has spoiled me as she always does on my birthday. She served me trout for breakfast and lunch. Tonight we will sit together by the fire in the *foglar friulano*, her new hearth, specially made by the local stonemason, while I recite my story.

"I was born under the city butcher shop in an old woven basket one September morning," I begin.

"*Bene, bene* Fortuna," complimented Luna as I finished my story. "No matter how many times I hear your story, I am amazed and grateful. You are a very special cat indeed. I am so blessed you are my friend. Now, it is time for *un regalo*, a gift."

"Luna," I said feeling embarrassed. "You did not need to give me a gift! You already treated me to fresh fish today; all I need is to be here, in our home with you, my best friend."

"Never you mind, Fortuna. I am excited to

give you *un regalo*," said Luna as she rose slowly from her chair. She climbed the spiral wooden stairs to her bedroom where she opened the drawer of the small table and lifted out a smooth olive wood box.

"Are your eyes closed, *mia piccola gatta nera*?" she called to me as she descended the stairs.

"*Sì, sì, sì*, Luna," I replied.

"*Bene*, let me sit down, then you may see what I have for you." Luna placed the box on the cushioned bench next to me. Her knees and the chair creaked a little as she sat. My ears twitched with excitement.

"You may open your eyes. *Buon compleanno*, happy birthday, Fortuna!"

I did not hesitate a moment. "*È bellissima*, it is beautiful! *Grazie*! I will keep treasures inside. Did you make it from one of the olive trees?"

"*Sì, sì, sì*, yes, of course, I did! Do you remember the branch Mario broke? Lorenzo carved this lovely box from that wood."

Luna and I looked at each other and laughed, remembering grouchy, lazy Mario.

"*Allora*, let's not talk of any unpleasantness on

your birthday because *mia piccola gatta nera*, there is more!" Luna's eyes were bright with excitement. Her smile seemed to fill the whole room. "Open the box," she said.

I was curious and surprised. "Luna, you are too kind to me."

I lifted the lid of the olive wood box with my left paw. Inside was a book. On the front cover was a painting of a black cat and a woman with black hair.

"*Sono io*! It's me! And you! Oh, Luna, what does it say?"

"It is your story, Fortuna. That is your name on the front. In the weeks after you returned home from the shepherd's house, I wrote your story. Each year after you share it with me on your birthday, I add details. Last year I was finally satisfied. Stella drew pictures, and Tomasso took it to a printer in *Venezia*," Luna explained.

"It is wonderful, Luna."

Purring loudly, I hopped into Luna's lap. I looked up at her and touched my nose to her chin. "How can I ever thank you?" I nuzzled closer to Luna as she wrapped her arms around me.

"*Prego,* you are welcome. It is my pleasure. I am the one who should thank you! You are my best friend. Our friendship brings me great joy. I thank God every day for bringing us together, saving you, and returning you home. He has always had a special plan for you. I am honored to be part of that plan."

Luna paused as a tear rolled down her wrinkled cheek. I licked the tear away. "Don't cry, Luna," I said softly as I rubbed my face on hers. "I am healthy and strong. I do not ever plan to leave you again."

"*Mia piccola gatta nera,* you know these are happy tears because I love you."

"I love you too, Luna."

Fine
The End

Afterword:
Our Cat, Lucky

In 2019 while my family and I were living in Aviano, Italy we met a young black cat in our tiny 300-year-old village. My mom named him Lucky, after her black rescue cat, Lucky Tarheel. Little did we know he would become our pet and shape our family in many beautiful, unexpected ways. I believe God brought us together so Lucky could rescue us and we could rescue him. For the record, I do not believe in luck; however, his name has proven to be highly appropriate.

Lucky befriended my younger son, Daniel, first. I used to see Lucky trotting along behind everyone who walked on our street, but he always ran to greet Daniel after school.

By mid-March 2020 when Italian law did not permit us to leave our property, even for exercise, Lucky began to come to us, and he basically never left. He played (and interrupted) games with us in our courtyard and frequented our second-floor balcony, making amazing leaps through narrow railings up from the stone wall dividing our courtyard and the neighbor's yard. Lucky was our virtual school mascot because he exhibited many qualities we were striving to have: friendliness, encouragement, and love. I included pictures and comments about Lucky in my R.A.R.E. (Roberts' Academy of Resilience and Encouragement) updates. Friends and family all over the world enjoyed reading about Lucky's antics in my frequent Facebook posts. He was not only bringing us happiness, but he was bringing smiles to others far away during a very stressful season.

On May 21st, three days after the first Italian lockdown ended, Lucky was following me and Daniel down our very narrow street when a passing car spooked him. He darted like a squirrel under the wheel of the car. I was instantly certain it was a fatal injury. I said a desperate prayer asking God to save him, but rationality immediately told me his brain injury was too severe for survival. Since Lucky was not our pet, I carried him to his house and tearfully passed his unconscious body to his owners. I then carried my hysterical and traumatized son home where we cried for hours.

Four very sad days later, to our grateful surprise, we found out Lucky was alive. We were shocked and elated. Lucky's fans worldwide were amazed too. His survival felt like a miracle.

Together with the generous support of Lucky's fans, we supported his surgeries and lengthy vet stay. When he was discharged seven weeks later, his owners graciously allowed us daily visits with him. Our reunion with Lucky will always be one of my most precious memories of our time in Italy.

Lucky was frightfully skinny, weak, lethargic, and worse, aloof. His vision in his left eye was impaired, causing him balance problems. He was alive, but he did not seem like the same cat. We sat quietly with him, petted him, and read to him.

"How much improvement is possible? Will he heal enough to be playful again? Does he know who we are?" I asked myself these questions daily and frequently told my boys, "I don't know." I did not have any answers. We had to wait and see, but deep down, I believed God would restore him to be the same sweet, fun, affectionate cat. Why else would He have saved this little street cat?

Over the next several weeks, the physical therapist in me started noticing minor improvements in Lucky's behavior. I was ecstatic the first time I saw him play with a grasshopper for two seconds and thrilled when he started walking toward us, not away as if we were invisible.

As Lucky continued to improve, he began escaping from his owner's house — he came to our courtyard every time he escaped. He *did* know who we were, and he wanted to be with us! In late July Lucky's owners gave him to us. We all knew he was not going to settle for anything less than being our pet, but new troubles were just beginning. I will simply share that for the remainder of our time in Italy, Lucky's original owners were unkind to us, and to him.

A few weeks later, I found Lucky on our balcony for the first time since his accident. His recovery exceeded all of my expectations. By the end of August, Lucky was 100% recovered, except for part of his left eye which remained cloudy until very recently. He purred, played, and surprised us with new shenanigans including entering into our house through the retractable window screens without disturbing the screen. We joked he was a cat burglar.

I often wished Lucky could talk to me, telling me the truth about where he was when he was missing from our house or what was truly happening during the many trials with our neighbors. If Lucky had been able to talk, he would have told me what we eventually learned: he needed our protection.

Despite ongoing issues with our neighbors, Lucky remained a happy cat. He worked his way inside our house, no longer needing to sneak in. He enjoyed sleeping on our beds, batting Christmas ornaments, jumping on the piano, pulling the alarm string in the Italian shower, playing soccer in the courtyard with chestnuts, licking the butter dish, and sitting with us while we read or watched Carolina basketball.

In July 2021 Lucky moved with us to America. He now enjoys the sweet and spoiled life of an indoor cat. His favorite place is our screened-in porch where he watches birds and takes naps in the sunshine.

We never knew a little black cat could bring us so much joy! We are forever grateful he chose us.

I hope Lucky and Fortuna's stories will remind you to see the beauty of love and friendship in every corner of your life.

With love and gratitude,

Katy and Lucky🐾

Lucky enjoying
the view
from our Italian
balcony.

Lucky relaxing on
the screened-in
porch in Virginia.

Discussion Questions

1. How has a pet or friend shaped your life story?

2. What story do you think your pet would share with you if he/she could speak?

3. How would you describe Fortuna in the early chapters? What is her main character flaw?

4. How did Fortuna's experiences in Portazzurro influence her decision to choose Luna?

5. Luna means moon, Fortuna means fortunate or lucky, and Speranzamonte means Hope Mountain. How are these names foreshadowed?

6. How did Fortuna's character transform during her travels and trials? What did she learn as a result of her injury?

7. What do you hope to read in the Luna and Fortuna series in the future? Do you have a fun idea? Please share your ideas with me via email! ksrobertspt@gmail.com

A "fairy house"
in the woods near my former house in Italy.

Acknowledgments

Thank you, God, for saving Lucky from the car accident and keeping him safe many times after that. He is such a blessing to our family. I am grateful you brought us together and that I can share his story.

Thank you so much, Uncle Dan Dye for beautifully illustrating this book. I enjoyed working with you again and watching my words come to life in color through your detailed paintings.

Thank you to my editors, Charlotte Roberts, Elder Wellborn, and Alex Valenti, for your time, suggestions, and careful eyes which helped me polish this story. *Grazie mille*, Charlotte and Alex, for your corrections of my horrendous Italian grammar.

Thank you to my young consultants for your wonderful creativity! Riley Evans (age 8) thought of the onomatopoeia describing the sound of bouncing chestnuts, Victoria McDonald (age 8) created the name Pudoia from a combination of her favorite Italian town names, Sadee Stoner (age 8) named

Luna's rooster, Piero, and Claire Baird (age 11) wrote the *movento spotstari* spell Luna uses to move objects.

Thank you to my Launch Team: Lauren Addams, Jan Auten, Dawn Bagnetto, Amy Beach, Marsha Carroll, Laurie Evans, Mary Finney, Sarah Farner, Victoria French, Bobbie Jo Glaze, Kelli Hernandez, Candi McKee, Andrea McDonald, Allie Randall, Charlotte Roberts, Anne Sloop, Sally Sloop, Maria St. Clair, Markee Stoner, Ashley Tarter, and Courtney Tompkins for social media book promotion assistance and for your many wonderful ideas.

Mark, James, and Daniel, thank you for giving me pats on the back about my writing, marketing, and designs. I love you each with my whole heart. I could not ask for a more awesome family.

Last but not least, *grazie mille* Lucky, our Italian superhero cat, for choosing us to be your family, for being incredibly adaptable since our move to America, and for being my muse.   I love you, *mio piccolo gatto nero*.

Introduction
My Adventures

Last summer I backpacked through Europe for six weeks. I saw places I had always dreamed of visiting. I toured ancient castles, saw famous monuments, and admired priceless art in world-renowned museums. I climbed narrow spiral stairs in bell towers and walked for hours along the cobbled streets of old cities. I soaked in as many new experiences as I could fit into each long summer day. I met and talked with interesting people from multiple countries, but by far, the most memorable friend I made was an elderly Italian woman with beautiful jet black hair named Luna.

I first learned about Luna in a magazine article. She was pictured in her olive grove and quoted as an expert on olive oil. I thought she had such a unique appearance and a fun twinkle in her eye, I knew my travels would be incomplete without meeting her. I searched for her address on the

1

internet, but I could not find it. Hoping to find her, I bought a train ticket to her town. Fortunately, as soon as I stepped off the train I saw a sign for her business.

I followed a series of these simple signs until I reached a large stone house with a gated garden.

When I arrived Luna was softly humming a mesmerizing tune while tending large tomato plants in her garden. "*Buongiorno,* good morning, Signora Luna," I said softly, not wanting to startle her. "I am eager to taste the best olive oil this side of Venice. May I come in please, *per favore*?"

"*Sì, sì, sì, yes!*" she said enthusiastically answered while motioning for me to enter the garden gate. "Taste it you will! *Entra per favore,* come in please. My olive oil is the best in this land! It is best enjoyed with good food. Good food is best enjoyed with good wine. Good wine is best enjoyed with a good story!"

With her enticing invitation, I was instantly filled with delight and curiosity. I was about to make a new friend I would never forget and hear a story I would still be retelling when I am old.

Chapter 1
The Olive Grove

A long time ago in northern Italy in the month of May, Mario was hungry and in need of work. He walked kilometer after kilometer, village after village, through the foothills of the Dolomite Mountains searching for good fortune. Mario was a very lazy man. His laziness caused him to lose a series of jobs, but he was also a very superstitious man. He believed his hardships were the result of breaking a mirror four years ago.

Mario's wealthy aunt who lived on the Grand Canal in Venice gave him the mirror for his birthday when he was a boy. In his teenage years, he admired himself in the mirror for hours every day as he dreamed about a bright future. But as his life became more and more unsettled, he struggled to be hopeful. He was convinced he had at least three more years of bad luck ahead of him before he would escape the curse of the broken mirror.

Mario trudged along filled with bitterness and

anger as he recollected his many lost jobs over the years. He was so grouchy when he entered a new village, he did not offer customary greetings such as *"Buongiorno."* Instead he loudly announced, "I need someone to give me a job chopping wood, carrying water from the river, or tending goats." Women hurried inside their homes and children hid when they heard his deep, bellowing, angry voice.

By Mario's fourth week of jobless searching, he was thin and exhausted. His broad shoulders sagged as he trudged onward cursing under his breath about his bad luck. His once young and handsome face, despite his rather large nose, grew angular from weight loss. His eyes even appeared smaller and less round because he glared angrily most of the time. His beard and mustache, brown with hints of red, were quite full. They could have been his best features, but they were unkempt. He saw his reflection from time to time in pools of water, but he no longer cared about his appearance as he once had.

Mario had almost given up hope of finding work and a better life when when he saw a steep, narrow, rocky path one evening. The trail was unmarked, but he felt compelled to follow it for a reason he could not explain. He continued until the path ended at an olive grove. The olive trees were very well tended; they were all pruned in the same shape and to the same height of about four meters. They grew in straight rows numbering thirteen in each row.

If Mario had counted the trees, he might not have entered the grove. He believed thirteen was an unlucky number, but he was too tired after a long day of walking to pay much attention to detail. The ground was covered in soft grass. Wild peonies and irises bloomed along the inside border of the perimeter stone wall. It was a lovely place. Mario, however, only saw it as a resting place for one night before continuing on his journey the next morning. As the sun disappeared behind the mountain and the colors of the evening sky faded into darkness, Mario reclined under a tree. He quickly fell into a fitful, hungry sleep.

Early the next morning, he woke to the constant calling of cuckoo birds on the mountain. "*Cuckoo…cuckoo…cuckoo*," sang the birds back and forth to one another. "*Basta! Basta!* Stop! I'll never get back to sleep with your noise!" he yelled. Frustrated and irritated, he slowly and stiffly rose, twisting and arching his broad aching back as he stood. "Maybe today will be my lucky day," he grumbled.

He picked a handful of small olives and

greedily ate them. They were hard and bitter. Olives are not ripe until autumn, but he was famished so he ate them anyway. Then he had more. He cursed loudly as he chewed the disgusting olives.

"*Basta! Basta*!" he shouted again toward the persistent birds while spitting bits of olives from his mouth. "Can't a man have breakfast in peace?" His booming voice echoed off the mountain like thunder.

Unsatisfied with the olives, Mario climbed a tree hoping to find a bird's nest full of eggs or something else more palatable to eat. Unfortunately, all he discovered was a large spider's web. He exploded with rage as the dewy web stuck instantly in his bushy mustache and knotted beard. As he furiously batted his face to remove the sticky web, the branch supporting him cracked.

With a loud snap the limb broke and fell, and so did Mario. Tree branches scratched him as he fell. One branch scraped across his right eye and deeply cut him from his cheek to his forehead. He was fortunate the branch did not injure his eye, but Mario felt anything but grateful.

He lay across the broken branch bleeding. He

crossly wondered how his day could get any worse when he noticed a short woman a meter away.

She stood on the opposite side of the low, white stone wall with one hand on her hip and the other on a long wooden staff. She peered intently and curiously at Mario with her sparkling dark eyes.

Mario stared back startled by her sudden arrival and confused by her contrasting features. He was not sure if she was a young woman or an old woman. She had long, wavy black hair that flowed over her shoulders and down her back in a youthful way, but her face and hands were extremely wrinkled.

About the Illustrator

Photo Credit: NC Red Cross

Dan Dye is the author's uncle and he is honored to illustrate her books. Dan grew up in Chapel Hill, North Carolina and has a degree in Sociology from the University of North Carolina at Chapel Hill. Dan has enjoyed art since early childhood. In high school, he nurtured his talents for painting and silversmithing. After retiring from a long career in sales, Dan has made silversmithing his second career. He lives in Raleigh, NC with his wife of fifty years. They have two grown daughters and two granddaughters. Through the years they have owned several black cats.

www.dandye.com

About the Author

Photo Credit: Reyna Truscott

Katy Sloop Roberts grew up in Virginia. She has a degree in English from the University of North Carolina at Chapel Hill and a master's degree in Physical Therapy from the University of Alabama at Birmingham. Katy has enjoyed writing since her grandparents gave her a lined journal for Christmas at age seven. *Fortuna Finds a Family* is her second book. As an Air Force spouse, she has lived in many U.S. states, Germany, and Italy. Currently, she lives in Yorktown, Virginia with her husband, two sons, and Lucky, the Italian black cat who inspired this book.

www.lunaandfortuna.com

Dear Readers,

I love hearing from you. Please visit my website and sign up for the Luna and Fortuna email newsletter so we can stay in touch, and I can share special offers and activities with you!

Your email correspondence, and your book reviews on Amazon, Goodreads, and other sites are sweet like my favorite German Chocolate birthday cake! Your words delight my senses and make my author heart smile.

Grazie, Katy

<u>www.lunaandfortuna.com</u>
Instagram: @lunaandfortuna
Facebook: Luna and Fortuna

You can read more about me in *Mario and The Stones!*